I0626027

Hellsong Series

Infidels: Cris

EXECUTION

SHAUN O. MCCOY

SISYPHEAN PUBLISHING

This is a work of fiction. The damnation portrayed in this novel is fictitious, and similarities between it and any actual damnation are strictly coincidental.

Execution

Editor-in-Chief: Gabrielle Olexa
Associate Editors: Kitty Garner, Andrew Anderson, Justin Williams

Title art: Dusan Arsenic
Title Layout: Paul Mavis

A Sisyphean Publishing Book

Http://hellsongseries.com

ISBN-13: 978-0692168714 (Sisyphean Publishing)
ISBN-10: 0692168710

First Edition September 2018

Printed in the United States of America

0 9 8 7 6 5

PRAISE FOR SHAUN O. McCOY AND THE HELLSONG SERIES

OTHER WORKS BY SHAUN O. McCOY

HELLSONG SERIES: ARTURIAN
Even Hell Has Knights
Knight of Gehenna
March Till Death
Book IV (2019)

HELLSONG SERIES: INFIDELS: CRIS
Affliction
Soulfall
Dust
Convalescence
Execution
Wasteland
Restoration

NOVELLAS
Electric Blues
Binary Jazz

This book is for Jami Conniff

Execution

the rest, its anemic branches laden with tangled masses of sinfruit vines. I watch as a flock of psychopomp sparrows flutters under the drooping limbs before soaring out across the chamber.

Though my son is the slightest among us, thin of frame and only around eight years old, they've assigned two guards to him. Damocles' sword, hanging by that metaphorical horsehair, is above his head, too.

Keith follows along with us, his stride uneven and lurching, his eyes wild and unfocused. If anyone is going to toss themselves into the endless abyss of mists and stone below, my money's on him.

"Escort one prisoner across to the Wicker Tree at a time," Amirani orders. "Chuck, Jacobs, you're responsible for getting their equipment to the Storage Tree."

The treemen obey, for some reason choosing not to lump him in with us convicts. Maybe I can understand why. As far as guidance goes, they've got a choice between Amirani or Keith—and no sane person would pick Keith.

Two men move to Aiden, one ahead, and the other behind. They lead him onto the bridge. My son doesn't hold the rope rail, though his captors do. I watch their crossing as sparrows fly above and below them. Their progress is slow by necessity, but is retarded further by the fear Aiden's guards hold toward him.

And of course they fear him. He's a monster after

all—just like his dad.

Amirani steps up to my right side and speaks to the guard on my left. "I'll prep the Tree Lord. Let him know we've taken them and their wight to the Wicker Tree."

The guard nods and his grip on my tricep tightens. "I'll let Fabian know after we drop them off."

Amirani grunts his approval.

My son is halfway across. Maybe he's out of range of the treemen's stone-tipped arrows. Since he's a wight, their bullets won't be able to hurt him. If he was going to fight and make a break for it, he'd do it when he reached the far side. But where the hell would he go? The only quick way out of this chamber is down, and wight or no, that fall would kill him.

"Fabian will visit your woman friend," the guard says to Amirani, nodding toward Cid. "You know he can't get it up without beating a girl. Doesn't that bother you?"

"I'd be lying if I told you no," Amirani says. "But it's Fabian's prison. What he does in the Wicker Tree is beyond my control."

Cid's tough. She can handle it. We're all going to die anyway. What's the worst he can do, beat her? Rape her?

But the latter thought raises the hackles on the back of my neck. I am the fool of my own impotent fury. I love that little girl, and in her own way, she loves me back. That means something to a man, infidel or no. It means I want to protect her. To keep her safe. To make sure what happened to me in Tintagel never happens to her. The idea of someone violating her in that way sends daggers stabbing into the tender parts of my heart.

I've not felt wounds like this since Myla.

"I'm sorry," the guard tells Amirani, his voice seeming genuinely disturbed.

They love him, that's obvious. Amirani has been fighting alongside them for some time, and as an infidel, doubtlessly he's saved many of their lives. I don't know if that's bought him enough goodwill to save Amirani from the Tree Lord's justice, but maybe—

"If you want," the guard lowers his voice to a whisper, "I can escort the woman infidel across. I can advise her to jump."

The daggers in my heart twist.

Amirani shakes his head. "No."

I see Cid's face and marvel at her beauty. At her green eyes and slightly upturned nose. At her fine elvenesque cheekbones. I want nothing more than to hold her close.

"I know you're hoping they'll be pardoned," the treeman says, "but surely you must know they'll be forced to take the fall."

I can practically feel that sword swaying over my head.

"It's the Tree Lord's decision," Amirani says. "We

can't make it for him."

"But you know what that decision will be," my guard presses.

I look at Amirani, at his stoic face.

"I know," he says, his voice calm and even.

Aiden makes it to the far side.

Amirani points to me. "Cris next."

I, apparently, only warrant a one guard escort.

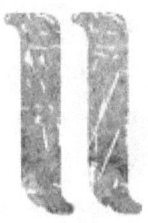

I become lightheaded as we move toward the center of the bridge.

A hand presses against my back and I jerk, nearly losing my balance.

"You're stalling," the guard accuses me.

A sparrow chirps from a nearby branch. I realize I'm breathing heavily—and I'm sweating enough to soak the armpits of my Icanitzu armor. Slowly, I turn to face the guard.

Someone calls out from the landing, but I ignore them.

I pause to catch my breath before speaking. "I'm not that kind of guy, either."

"I'm not stupid," the treeman says. "You're an infidel. I know you could take that gun from my belt and shoot me with it. But they'll kill you." He jerks a thumb over his shoulder.

With the back of my sprained hand, I wipe sweat from my brow. "Man, believe me. I ran a marathon to get here, and capped it off with a mile-long climb. I'm about one leg cramp away from tumbling off this thing. You've got to give me a bit of leeway here."

He sneers suspiciously and takes a few steps back.

"Move along!" someone shouts from the landing.

Neither the guard nor I move.

I look ahead across the chamber and see the hole in the Wicker Tree where they'd taken my son.

"You're wrong, you know," I tell him.

The guard takes another step back, his hand inching nervously toward the gun at his belt. "About what?"

"About the Tree Lord sending us to our deaths," I tell him. "You've sided with the wrong guys. Our wight's been tamed. His brain is fried. Keith is working with a wight too, and it's not tame. It kills."

He grins and takes a confident step toward me. "I thought all infidels were as good as Amirani, but you're pathetic. Keith had a wight with him, you're right about that, but only because he captured it from the Archdevil Varadoolyn. He gave us the creature so we could try to extract information on the Archdevil's whereabouts."

Varadoolyn? Who the hell is that? And Keith turned Durgan in? Captured from an Archdevil? What the hell is going on here? How much went on while I was recovering in the safe chamber?

Just one time, just for one fucking time, I'd like to know what the hell is going on.

"Keep walking, infidel," he says. "Whatever game you've been playing is over. Justice is the only thing you've got left. Justice, and a long fall."

There's a smile twitching at the corners of his mouth. He's enjoying my misery. Maybe we humans really are evil. Maybe Hell is something we really do deserve.

The Wicker Tree's landing is broader than most, and it circles halfway around the tree. There's a tremendous hollow in the trunk, like the kind where an old world owl might have lived—except scaled up in size to match the insane size of the tree. Its opening gapes before me, carved wooden steps lead down through the hollow, disappearing into the blackness within.

Women gather sinfruit from the vines which hang from the trunk and branches above. The smell of sap is strong but holds no comfort for me.

"Go on down," the treeman says.

I turn. He's got his gun drawn. In the distance I see they've started taking Q across.

I descend onto the hollow's stairs. It becomes dark almost immediately. I smell something decaying, but it's not altogether unpleasant—like rotting wood. I put my foot down into the blackness, counting on the regularity of the steps. That, at least, doesn't let me down.

My eyes adjust quickly, and now there's enough light coming from a passage ahead to illuminate the edges of the stairs.

That passage opens off to my right as I go down. Iron bars, partially rusted, form a wall which separates us from the level beyond. A little light spills into the level from a few openings to the outside, but these are also barred. Shadowy shapes of stumbling men move in the dim light.

Corpses.

Oh hell.

"Keep on moving," the treeman says.

I remember Amirani talking to us about the undead when we traveled through Dendra earlier. They kept corpses here so they could use their corpsedust to ferment their alcohol. Maybe I can have some bloodwater with my last meal—assuming they'll even bother to feed us.

"Here," my guard says as we make it to the next level. The stairs keep going down, spiraling into the blackness beneath me.

This level is slightly better lit, and is home to

several cubbies. Their openings are blocked by evenly spaced bars. Unlike their cousins on the floor above, their iron is unrusted. The cells on the left don't have windows so much as their back walls are completely missing. In their stead are more bars, and beyond that, Dendra's open chamber.

There's no door into any of the cells, so I have no idea how the hell they plan to get my ass in one of them.

Right by the staircase is a series of pulleys whose chains run vertically down into the trunk.

A man waits there. Maybe he's our warden.

"Second cell on the left," the pulleyman says.

He begins tugging on one chain and three of the bars on the cell they've marked out for me begin to rise into the trunk. The sound of tinkling bells accompanies their ascent.

The iron bars stop about three feet up.

I walk forward, dreading the stretching of my taut muscles. There is a prisoner in the first cell on the right, already. His skin is pale, no, paler than pale, and blue veins run through it like marble. He looks at me with his all black eyes.

Durgan. That fucker.

He stands as I walk down the hallway, his obsidian eyes glinting in the dim light. After gaining his feet, he remains motionless. I can only guess that his irisless eyes are looking at me.

"Good to see that you're well," I tell him.

"Move on," says the treeman. "Get in your cell."

Aiden is in the first cell to the left, opposite Durgan, sitting cross-legged in the middle of the floor. His black eyes are similarly implacable.

"We'll be okay, son," I tell him.

As if to expose my lie, the treeman grabs me harder by the tricep and forces me down to my knees.

"Crawl," he orders.

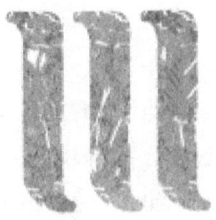

Hours pass slowly.

The bars are secure. Hell, they're more than secure. Originally, someone must have drilled holes into the floor and the ceiling to install them, and at that point, they might have been loose enough to pry out. Unfortunately, the tree has healed around them, locking the iron in tight.

Well, that's true for all but three of the bars, but they are an exception in name only. Those are the bars which the pulleyman can retract up into the trunk. If you fuck with them, the bells chime, and you get a very angry guard with a shotgun pointed at you. As the infidels say, I know this empirically.

I doubt even a Minotaur could break out of this prison.

They've left me in my Icanitzu armor, probably because they don't know what the hell it is, so I figure I can survive the first few blasts if I need to—until they learn to go for my head.

The entire back wall of my cell is open to the Dendra chamber beyond—except for the bars, of course—but even so, not much light makes it in here. The vines on the Wicker Tree provide some very effective shade, and there are some thick branches and a platform below, blocking the bright mists. Ironically, when the chamber is dimming and the mist is just thick enough to be seen outside, my cell is at its brightest.

My son is located to my right, and I've shared a few short words with him, leaning up against his wall and whispering. Q is to my left. He's sleeping now, but as soon as he wakes up, I plan to ask him about this Varadoolyn. Catty-corner on my right, when I look out into the hallway, I can see Durgan. He's on constant alert. Whenever a guard walks by, Durgan's head follows.

Straight across from me is Neb, and catty-corner to my left is Cid.

Infidels like alternatives. They need choices to thrive, opportunities to take advantage of. They like to lure their enemies into hostile environments. They like to do all kinds of shit that is just fucking impossible to pull off in a prison cell. And me escaping, that'd just be the beginning. I'd have to somehow get Cid and Q and Neb and my boy out too.

Well, I *guess* I could live without Neb, but it would be pretty bad form at this point.

I move back to the outside bars. If I can somehow knock one loose, I could probably climb the tree. Or I could leap and catch some of the vines out there and land on the branches below. They might absorb my fall a little.

I reach my good hand up through the bars and feel the tree trunk just above my cell.

The bark feels rough but is firm enough to get a good grip on.

Then I hear feet shuffling. A cold, dry hand grabs mine.

I try to pull my arm back but the icy grip holds me. I feel teeth on my thumb, so I jerk to one side. Then I jump up, my sore legs burning, and let my weight pull my arm down. My hand slips out and I fall to the ground.

God my muscles hurt.

A small, thin line of corpse dust descends, slowly falling outside my cell.

I hear some laughter from the guards. "I think he met one of the upstairs neighbors."

Fuck, the corpses are above.

Well, I should be able to climb up and around them

if I can ever get past these bars.

It's clear that our best chance is for Cid to try convincing the Tree Lord that we're in the right, but what are the odds on that? I sit down by the bars, take my thumbnail and start working at the wood around one's base.

It's quite possible the tree will heal itself faster than I can wear it away. Still, I've got shit else to do.

My attempt is futile, I find. The weak link here turns out to be my thumbnail. It's getting abominably sore.

"Cris, can you hear me?" Q's voice comes to me through the wall.

"Yeah." I say.

"Is that Durgan, in the cell over there?"

"It is."

His sardonic chuckle is deep, and I practically feel it vibrating the wood between us. "You doing alright?"

I thought about this. "I don't know, am I?"

There is a long pause. "No, Cris. None of us are doing alright. By lying on our first trip through Dendra, we wasted some much needed trust. I don't know that we'll have any leverage left."

"I'm working on the bars now," I say.

"Yeah, how's that going?"

"Like shit."

He chuckles again. "Your thoughts are those of a free man, Cris. If you want peace, you must think the thoughts of a prisoner."

"I don't know if this is the right time for that Zen infidel shit. I just got free from Keith, and . . . man, we have to get out of here."

"Agreed, but be careful. If your escape options have a very low chance of success, you might want to wait and see if Cid can talk us out of trouble first."

I put my fingers on the wall, feeling the grain of the wood. "And even if I can get out, I still need to find a way to get you free."

"Remember this one thing, Cris. It is better that one of us lives than all of us die. I don't know if that's what's about to happen. I don't know if your escape attempt will completely ruin any diplomatic solution."

"Q!" I say a little too loudly. I control myself, and lower my voice. "I can't abandon you, not after all you've done for me."

He doesn't respond.

"I won't leave without Aiden," I say.

I can almost hear him thinking that if I had just done the right thing and killed my son, we wouldn't be prisoners here.

And Q's right.

Fuck. Cid *has* to be able to convince the Tree Lord we're in the right. I mean, Keith is a dead giveaway, right? He's about to crack.

She'll save us.

She has to save us.

I hear the sound of gunfire outside.

"The hell?" I come up to my feet, surprised at the agony in my sore muscles.

I see Cid come to her bars. Neb is alarmed as well. Only Durgan remains calm.

"Easy, Cris," Cid says. "Dendra is under attack, but Amirani says this happens fairly often. It isn't likely to fall." She cocks her head to one side. "I hear dyitzu fire."

There are more gunshots, and some soldiers are shouting. I keep hoping the sounds will stop . . . but they don't. The fighting continues. It's more than just a handful of dyitzu.

"Can Callodax, or the infused, or whatever he is, control devils?" I ask Cid.

She puts one of her tiny hands to the bars. "It's possible. Because the spiders and the pigmaditz attacked his men, it didn't look like he could control them. To be honest though, we don't know if Callodax was even there. He might also have been able to strike a deal with a Minotaur or Icanitzu Lord. They could control the devils on his behalf."

My gut is screaming that the infused is behind this attack. Dendra might survive small raids from devils, but I can't imagine them standing up against Callodax.

A fireball rushes by my bars and buries itself in a set of sinfruit vines.

I overhear one guard talking reassuringly to the

other. "It's okay, Josh, your family is in the Safe Tree. Those defenses are very strong. They'll be fine."

I limp two steps over to the internal bars. "We can help," I shout at the guards. "Give us guns and we can help."

They're clearly very nervous and are looking out through one of the empty cells at the end of the hall.

I hear my son's voice.

"What?" I call back to him.

"Stay away from the window, Cris. You don't want to get burned."

IV

I hear the hisses of the dyitzu fireballs as they coast through the air—then I feel vibrations in the floor as they impact with the Wicker Tree. Sometimes I see the missiles sweeping across the bar-interrupted panorama. Many hit the vines, splashing their liquid fire across them, wilting green leaves and charring the grey sinfruit. Occasionally entire vines curl up in the flames. If the dyitzu break in, I'll be helpless. They'll be able to pelt me with fire through the bars, and there will be nothing I can do to fight back.

On their own, the devils could never kill us, but these damn treemen have done most of the work for them.

The smoldering fruit smells like burnt marshmallows.

It seems unfair that the scent, previously associated with my fondest memories of the old world, has to be superimposed upon this living nightmare.

I hear the shouts of soldiers as they run back and forth from tree to tree. I hear the booms of their guns and the screams of the wounded and the dying. I hear the rush of steam as treemen pour buckets of water on burning wood. Through gaps in the walls of vines, I see the soldiers take up positions in protected wicker nests. Each nest is reinforced with thick wooden planks, and they often have openings so their soldiers can shoot out of them.

But not all the wicker-helmed treemen have guns; some fight with bows and arrows. I see a nest under attack now, streams of dyitzu fire pelting the wicker and wood structure.

Other soldiers run into our prison from time to time, whispering in desperate, short sentences to our guards. They point franticly as they speak, as if toward locations in the battle.

I watch Durgan, the marble man, focus on each guard.

The thing I hate about Durgan's eyes is that he can be staring at me, at any time, and there's no way for me to know. Sometimes, because of the way his head moves, I think I know what he's looking at—but I can't be sure.

The devils won't kill him when they break in here, that's for damn sure. They'll let him loose. On the bright side, that goes for my son as well.

I walk up to my bars and motion to the guard. It's the same treeman who guided me into my cell. Warily, he approaches me. He stops before my door, a wisp of his blond hair protruding from a gap in his wicker helmet. His weight is on his back foot, as if he's afraid to get near me.

"If it comes to it," I tell him, motioning to the stairs, "and the devils arrive here, you know you can free us, and we'll fight for you."

He takes a half-step backward. He chews on his lip, and his eyes focus on the floor while his mind tries to process this idea.

Slowly, as if some terrible nightmare is taking over his thoughts, his face contorts into a grimace of fear. "Is this Varadoolyn?" he asks me. "Will we lose?"

I feel the hackles rise on the back of my neck.

This man clearly has respect for me now. I replay the conversation we had on the bridge, and think of his disdain. I remember my responses. What's changed?

He's afraid.

And I'm an infidel as far as he's concerned. That counts for something, even in this godforsaken tree cubby.

But oddly, he's right to ask me. I know the force

which is behind this attack . . . I think. I never saw the infused controlling demons, but I can't imagine this assault wasn't in some way his doing.

Well, maybe I shouldn't be so sure. This could be a result of our actions. We riled up those devils pretty badly as we fought our way into Dendra.

"Have there been any humans in the assault yet?" I ask.

He shakes his head.

"Then you'll probably survive this one," I tell him.

He nods. "If they come, I'll make sure you have a chance to fight."

I reach out my hand. He steps back quickly, as if terrified I might break him.

I see Cid stand up, looking at me, her expression unreadable from across the dim room. Tentatively, he reaches out.

His friend steps forward. "Josh! Don't!"

But the treeman, Josh, takes my hand. We shake through the bars.

I let him go. Josh, a little unsteady on his feet, returns to his post by the gears.

Durgan is staring at me, I'm sure of it. I meet his black-eyed gaze.

That's right, motherfucker. If worse comes to worst, and your friends come to rescue you, you're not going to be able to murder me in this God damned bird cage.

If I'm lucky, I might just be able to murder you.

Long moments of quiet are interrupted by quick bursts of hisses, yells, and the booms of firearms. My mind drifts, connecting thoughts to each other in ways that, were I fully alert, would seem nonsensical.

I think I slept, but it's hard to be sure.

It's dark outside. The mists are thick and the light is dim. A ruddy glow illuminates the air outside, coming from the dying fires of dyitzu perhaps, or maybe the torches lit by treemen—or quite possibly from both.

The guards sit, two barely perceptible shadows in the prison hall, their backs to us.

A woman approaches, her bare feet making no noise on the wooden stairs. She walks between the guards, unmolested.

It's so dark I can't make out any of her features, but her shape, her shape I can see. Her hips do not switch back and forth as she moves. Rather, she steps toe to heel—like a dancer. She's carrying something, a basket I believe. The distant firelight from outside touches her as she approaches the bars, and I can tell she has red hair.

Myla?

No, Myla's dead. This woman is slightly broader and more busty. She kneels at the edge of my cage, and I can see her face and smell the sweet scent of tree sap. In her arms she carries a wicker basket.

I recognize this woman.

We passed her the first time we walked through Dendra. She'd been gathering sinfruit.

"You're here to feed me?" I whisper.

Her half-shadowed face nods very slightly.

"How the hell did you get stuck with this gig?" I ask.

She smiles. "Feeding you isn't so bad." She motions to her basket. "You should see the shit I have to give the wights."

I begin to stand as an infidel does, posting one arm and swinging my leg out to come to all fours, but then I think better of it, and move toward her on my knees. The way I do so is reminiscent of a wrestling shoot they'd taught me. I hadn't realized that such a short time spent training could entrench their movements so deeply within me. It's as if I'd always known how to move this way, and they'd just unlocked it.

The shadow of my head covers her chin, but I get a good look at her features for the first time. Her eyes are blue, their pupils wide to the point of blotting her irises out. Her hair is a little tangled and falls just past her shoulders. And her skin, her skin is as pale as my son's, smooth as marble, and seemingly as soft as a baby's. Even in shadow, I can tell her breath is coming quickly. I know the look she's giving me. This woman wants me.

It's a shame my ass is in here.

Then again, that may be the only reason she finds

me attractive. It's conceivable she noticed me as much as I noticed her on my last trek through here, but I find it much more likely she has a thing for bad men. And the fact that I'm an infidel, well, that has to do something.

"What's on the menu?" I whisper.

She looks over her shoulder, guiltily, as if she's not supposed to speak to me. But those guards are focused on listening for devils. If I had a way to escape this damn place . . .

But I don't.

And I sure as hell wasn't going to take this girl hostage.

She turns back to me quickly, as if emboldened by the negligence of the shadow-covered guards. "I just want you to know that I understand."

Her voice is low and has the hint of a southern accent. Even though I didn't have the first clue what the fuck she was talking about, I was happy to hear those words.

"Understand what?" My voice is soft, softer than the distant solitary hiss of a dyitzu fireball.

"I had a child once, and I . . . I couldn't give her up either. I just. I know you'll fall for your crime, but I . . . I want you to know that I understand."

Finally, a break. This is a woman I can work with.

"I need to save him," I say.

Her eyes widen, and empathy is written clearly in

them.

"I think . . ." She pauses for a second, her lips just barely parted. "I think that you two will get to die together."

Rage builds up inside me like bile. I choke it down.

"That's something," I whisper back.

She reaches her hand through the bars and touches me. "For the moment, you're safe. As long as the devils keep attacking, the King won't call court. And, well, it keeps Fabian busy, too."

She looks over her right shoulder toward Cid.

"Fabian's a leader?" I ask.

She nods, and her lip curls up into a sneer. "He's the general. He also rules the Wicker Tree. Your little black-haired friend is his type."

You'd think, having found ourselves surrounded by enemies, we humans would have enough sense to band together. But we're not that kind of species. Well, the infidels are, but the rest of us . . .

She pulls her hand back out of the bars and reaches into her basket. She produces some devilwheat bread and a few slices of sinfruit.

"If you eat quickly," she says, "I can give you some water. Normally we have to give you water before you eat, and it drives the prisoners crazy—but we might have time."

She glances over her shoulder at the guards.

I didn't really need any incentive to eat quickly. I

wolf down my food in a very, very uninfidel-like manner. She holds up what looks like a hound bladder. I open my mouth and lean against the bars. She pours the water into my mouth.

It must have been kept in a barrel, or in a tree, because I can taste the wood in the water. A little bit spills over my face.

I hear distant shouts and more gunfire.

She stands, turning toward the exit. I stand as well. The shots continue for a moment, then die down.

"For your sake," she says, and then she nods to Cid's cage, "and hers, I hope this attack lasts forever."

"But not for your sake," I say.

She shakes her head. "Maybe we deserve this."

That was anger, not guilt.

"What did they take from you?" I ask her quickly.

Her eyes are wide, and a flash of fear crosses her face. Then she regains her composure.

"Be well," she tells me.

Then she walks over to Q's cage.

I awaken to Durgan's voice, the stuff of nightmares. "Those were lies."

As if to remind me of my time recovering in Maylay Beighlay, my back locks on me when I try to sit up. And I'd thought I was sore yesterday.

Jesus Christ.

But for some reason, despite its intensity, the pain feels different to me somehow — disconnected. I pull my knees up to my chest and roll my back against the floor. Slowly, those muscles ease. I'm as sore now as I've ever been. I feel the tightness of my hamstrings just from raising my knees. My abdomen is on fire. There is a strange pain coming from my nipples as well. I remember they'd been bleeding from the long run we'd made.

And my arms are similarly useless from the climb.

Who'd have believed I could run so far? My body, apparently, is still in disbelief.

"My father *did not lie*," Aiden answers him.

Metaphorical alarm bells go off in my head, because when Aiden talks about his father, he's not talking about me.

He's talking about Xyn.

Q had explained to me the delicate balance of confusion and untruths which causes Aiden to be good. Xyn had preached that the quickest end to a man's damnation is to give up and give in to the evil. To resist, in Aiden's view, is to suffer. To acquiesce to the forces of damnation is to achieve peace.

While Aiden was alive, such a belief served to make him evil as he sought to hurry humanity toward death and inaction. Now, however, as a wight, the brainwashing has the opposite effect. Aiden *wants* people to suffer, so he wants them to fight, to resist Hell. It's like one of those double negative puzzles from the old world. Aiden doesn't, doesn't want people to be well.

If Durgan can unravel any single thread from that delicate web of lies the Archdevil used to turn my living son into a weapon of evil, my wight son might just become a weapon of evil. How's that for fucking ironic.

I assume Xyn would have slowly peeled away the illusions as Aiden continued his journey toward being a wight. Hell, considering Aiden was at least halfway there when I rescued him, the process had no doubt already begun. I'd have hated to watch that set of adolescent angst.

And this is a hell of a time for Aiden to go evil. I mean, honestly, any time would be soul crushing, but right now, right *fucking now*, our very lives depend on Aiden being able to convince the Tree Lord that he's a good wight.

The worry, the adrenalin, the fear—they loosen my muscles a little.

Carefully, I sit up.

Aiden's pacing bootsteps are dull thuds against the wood. There's a fight still going on in some distant tree, but the shouts barely carry.

"The infidels are not stupid," Durgan says. "If it were the case that dying relieved suffering, they would be killing people."

Is that true? Would we?

"They *are* stupid." Aiden spits the words. "They know nothing."

That's right, son, don't fucking trust your elders. We don't know shit.

I can't see Durgan from where I'm sitting, but I do see Cid. She's not looking at me, but she's extremely alert.

She knows how much danger we're in.

But what can we do? Can I help Aiden out? Almost anything I say will be a transparent lie.

"They are not fools," Durgan says. "One of them killed Xyn."

"Xyn predicted his own death," Aiden proclaims. "He said he would be reborn."

Xyn would say that shit. A man goes to Hell, hoping for a decent damnation, and the Archdevil he gets is a storefront apocalyptic prophet.

Durgan's laugh is low, hollow, and mocking. "He was to be reborn as your half-brother, coming out of your Mother. Tell me, is Myla able to give birth now?"

I await Aiden's answer, but one doesn't come.

Fuck.

I think I might be able to stand. I try to loosen my screaming muscles by stretching out my legs and sitting forward, reaching for my toes. Those toes, hidden under Jessica's well-made boots, are woefully far away.

Durgan speaks again. "And they know of the other levels of Hell."

"They do not!" Aiden says. "They cannot. No one has ever come back from Sheol."

"But they have," Durgan retorts. "The Infidel himself has returned from Sheol. And the Archdevil Tu El came from there. He has brought word from beyond the Erebus. Each death humans face brings them *more* pain. Each succeeding Hell is worse than the last. There may indeed be a point beyond our horizon of knowledge, of deaths beyond deaths, where a soul might be so tortured as to lose its identity, but that is the only way that one can say a person's torture stops."

With my sore arm propped up against the side of the wooden wall, I come to my tender feet. I'm lightheaded, and the room spins, but I'm standing.

"Xyn is Satan," Aiden says. "He told us so."

"You were flesh, then, not stone!" Durgan's voice rises. "He told you what you needed to hear. Were you then as you are now, he would certainly have told you this."

"My father does not lie!" Aiden's high-pitched voice betrays his insecurity.

Durgan is winning. That Sword of Damocles, it spins on its breaking thread, hovering just over us.

I try walking. My calves are so sore that they won't let me take a normal step. I have to keep my feet flat as I hobble toward the bars.

Cid's jaw is set. She points at me.

I hear joyful shouts of distant treemen, celebrating some victory or another.

"Did Xyn not say he would be reborn?" Durgan continues. "He certainly lied. He lied to fleshlings every day. Xyn learned of Hell from Tu El. Xyn was not a god. He told humans that to cow them. But Xyn died. And you know Archdevil souls do not travel to Sheol. He has been expunged. He has faced oblivion."

I need to save my son from this assault before he breaks. I take in a deep breath and prepare to lie. The lie comes easily to my mind because the infidels have taught me how this works, because at some time— perhaps in my struggle to reach Soulfall and save my son, or perhaps in the time we spent in the haven—a part of me had come to fear that my own beliefs are lies. That maybe there is no God. That there might never be, can never be, some final redemption. That there can never be some final battle at the end of days that will save me from my forever night. It will only get darker, and darker and darker.

Tears form in my eyes as I prepare to deceive my only son.

"Aiden," I begin, "did Xyn ever say *where* he would be reborn?"

I meet Durgan's black gaze as I hobble along the wall, getting as close to the pair as my cell will allow and gripping the cold iron bars for support. Bells tinkle lightly for a second in the distance.

"He did not," Aiden's high voice responds.

"And devils do not go to Sheol," I say, "but the seed of Xyn was in your mother's belly?"

Durgan's black eyes widen.

That's right, motherfucker, I know how to play this game. I was bred on it. They preached to me this reborn savior bullshit since I was a babe. I practically sucked it out of my mother's tit. I have no problem vomiting it back up.

"Cris' aim in this conversation is clear," Durgan counters.

"Is there something you're afraid I'm going to say, nonbeliever?" I strike back.

He raises his chin.

"Aiden, is that right?" I ask. "Was Myla pregnant when she died?"

"She was," Aiden spits. "When you killed her. When you ruined everything—"

"Bullshit!" I shout back. "I'm just a man, I cannot kill a god . . . unless he wanted me to."

Durgan's lips curl into a sneer.

Aiden doesn't answer.

I press on. "Archdevils don't go to Sheol, but what about half-devils? What about the soul in Myla's belly?"

"I don't know," Aiden says.

"If Xyn is *the* Devil, then he wouldn't just come in corporeal form to one Hell, Aiden. He'd come to them all. And he wouldn't have let his soon-to-be-mother die, or die himself, for no reason."

Honestly, it shocks me that this shit is even believable. I mean, really? Christ went through the charade of a crucifixion just to have a convenient excuse to pardon some sins and go meet his daddy? Xyn got himself impregnated in my ex-girlfriend and then suffered an abortion-a-la-Cris in order to go to Sheol? Fuck, if he was Satan, he could just *walk* there. But these sorts of things are believable to a tainted mind.

"You think he used you?" Aiden asks me.

I choose my next words very carefully. "Son, I don't know. I don't know much of anything. I just know that I'm not a very good infidel. You've seen how much better Q and Cid are than me. Do you think I could have killed Xyn? On my own?"

Of course I could. I planned my battlefield. I tricked him into bathing in his only weakness, and I got a little lucky. But if there's one thing I can count on Aiden doing, it's doubting my abilities.

He gets that from his mother.

"No," Aiden says. "I don't think you could. Durgan even said that Xyn had killed infidels before."

If my son buys this, will he be able to love me? Will he blame me for killing his mother and father if it was all predestined from the beginning?

Perhaps not. But there were Christians who blamed the Jews for deicide while simultaneously maintaining Christ's death was a suicidal sacrifice, so you never know.

Fuck Damocles, you can call me Judas.

"Were you lying?" I ask Durgan. "Was Xyn not powerful enough to face infidels?"

The marble man knows better than to lie now. "Xyn did slay infidels. But one of them had intuited a way to pass Xyn's immunities. Cris came armed with the knowledge that Xyn could be harmed with lightrock."

I'm struck by why infidels must be so damn annoying to demons. We are, in essence, a giant forum to share and keep knowledge. And we breed like fucking rabbits. Kill one of us, and Cid trains two more. One misstep, and the whole lot of us knows how to kill you.

"So I just happen," I say, "after years of searching, to find Xyn right after he impregnates Myla. And then, magically, I learn of his weakness and slay everyone at just the right time to send his soul to Sheol?"

Hey, that sounded pretty good. If I hadn't just made up the whole Xyn needs to go to Sheol shit a second ago, I might even have believed it myself.

"If Xyn wanted to go to Sheol," Durgan says, "he could have gone there without dying."

I snort. "Who are you to question the way Xyn does things? Like I said, I don't know. Aiden, maybe Durgan's right. Maybe I did kill Xyn all on my own. Maybe I did banish his soul to oblivion. But that baby, your half-brother, that might be Xyn. He might be in Sheol now, readying to return. But I didn't know your father, son. Not like you knew him."

"The infidel lies to you," Durgan's voice is calm again. "He knows that if you learn the truth, you'll turn against him. Are you really going to side with this monster who killed your father? Who killed your mother? This human who wants to change Hell into a paradise? To see all men happy? To see babies laughing and evil men punished?"

I look over to Cid. She had pointed at me. She didn't want a stalemate, she wanted a win.

"Neither I nor Durgan know the truth," I say, "at least not for certain. I was Xyn's enemy, and Durgan was just his henchman. But you, you were something different. You were his son, and Myla was his lover. Only you two knew the truth. You are the ones he'd really confide in. You loved him, didn't you? In your heart. Was he a liar? Search within yourself. Your heart knows the truth."

"You—" Durgan begins.

"Quiet!" Aiden shouts, cutting him off. "I need to think."

"It's—" Durgan tries again.

"Shut up!" Aiden's high voice is full of pain.

I hear some shuffling. Maybe my son's kneeling down. Maybe he's closing his eyes. Maybe he's looking deep into his soul. For a moment, I hear him whispering, but I cannot make out the words.

Aiden is praying. He's praying to the Devil for guidance. That's on you, Myla. That shit ain't on me.

"Durgan," Aiden shouts. "You're a liar! You should have known. You served with my father, you heard what he said, but you've closed your eyes to the truth. I know the truth, Durgan. I can *feel* it."

I grin as Durgan turns to me, his black eyes

narrowed in anger and his sneer is plastered on his marble face.

That's right, motherfucker. Try arguing with that shit. I limp slowly back to the outward-facing bars and look out to the vine-covered canopy.

"You can feel things are true in your heart," Durgan is saying, "but still be mistaken."

But the attempt is laughable. Xyn brainwashed my son. Durgan could talk himself hoarse, he could level untold amounts of logic and reason at the problem and it wouldn't do shit. Aiden has his feelings, his intuition, his heart.

I grin as I imagine Durgan banging his head into the brick wall that is my son's faith.

Sparrow chirps serenade me for half an hour before I realize what they mean.

The devils are gone.

The attack has stopped.

The sword is falling.

My body is a fucking wreck.

I might not even be able to walk all the way to the Tree Lord when he calls for us. My back is locking up again, so I roll on it as I did before to get some relief. Then I set about stretching my muscles. It doesn't do much, but it might be enough to keep them from turning into rocks.

Hopefully when I explain to the Tree Lord what the

hell happened, he'll understand. Their fucked up laws are their own. I never consented to follow them. It's not like I actually . . .

. . . did anything . . .

. . . wrong.

Wait.

Do I deserve this?

The memory of Myla shouting at me, reaching out for me, begging for mercy, hits me—flooding into my mind with a tidal wave of self-hate.

And those men I'd murdered.

It's not like I've done much better since then, either. I teamed up with a necromancer, failed to save my son, and then kept him alive as a wight with my lies.

Holy fuck. Am I the bad guy?

I'm sorry, Myla.

Maybe I drove her to evil. Maybe she was okay on her own. Maybe it was my weaknesses which turned her into what she became.

If they kill me, I won't have a shot at redemption.

But redemption is a Christian idea. It involves my sins being absolved. It's not something that really exists. Sin isn't real, or so the infidels teach. Only the evil acts themselves are. Nothing can undo them. There's no taint in my soul that can be expunged. I'm just . . . I'm just me.

But Cid *had* talked about redemption. She believed in it, or some form of it. A kind I've never really thought about before. What can make a bad man good? What can I do to transcend the absolutely horrific mess I've made of this?

I close my eyes and let the nightmares take me.

The sounds of heavy boots on the solid wooden steps wake me. They're coming for us. Our guards are looking expectantly toward the stairs. I see the face of the treeman I know best, the one that escorted me here. Josh is his name. Is it his shift again already? How long was I out?

He turns to me.

I expect a smug expression, but his face is wrought with worry. His mouth has curled downward, his lips twitching slightly. His eyebrows are lowered. His eyes are filled with—is it sorrow? Guilt? I can't tell.

I get the feeling we're not being taken to the Tree Lord. Something worse is happening. Our justice, will it be interrupted? Will we be dragged to the fall without having a chance to defend ourselves and then be tossed down into the mists we spent so long crawling out of?

Two wicker-helmed guards, each armed with AK-47s and sporting white cloaks, walk in from the stairwell and take up positions flanking the entrance. A helmetless bearded man with a mane of bright red hair enters, a green cape spread out across his broad shoulders. He's tall enough to need to duck under the overhang.

"General Fabian," Josh says, saluting.

"I've come to take stock of the prisoners." Fabian's voice is somehow both deep and nasal at the same time.

Josh motions to our cages. "The infidels are yours, General."

"You may leave," Fabian says.

Oh fuck.

Josh shakes his head. "You know our orders are—"

Fabian brushes by him, looking across the cells. I seek to meet his eyes, but Fabian isn't interested in me.

"Jake, Simon, get the guards out," he orders.

Josh doesn't put up a fight. He gives me one look, and I'm sure now that it's a guilty one, before marching up the stairs. His friend is close on his heels.

Fabian doesn't bother with the wights, or me or Q or Neb. He stops, his back angled to me, looking into Cid's cage, his red hair spilling in almost effeminate curls over his ridiculously broad cape-covered back.

Cid was dumb enough to count me as a friend, and look what I've dragged her into. I remember how tender she was when she'd been sleeping with me. It was her love that brought me back from the edge of the stilling.

Fabian turns his head to speak with his returning guards, and I see his face in profile. His jaw juts comically forward, the effect exaggerated by his bushy beard. His hook nose looks ludicrous in profile. I want to break that nose.

"Come here," Fabian's nasal voice intones, and then he turns back to Cid. "Strip, or my men will shoot you down."

I feel the ghost fingers of Melvin crawling down my skin, and my insides tighten as I remember what Igraine had made him do to me.

The pair of Fabian's guards raise their assault rifles.

I hobble over to the bars and grip them with my shaking hands.

Q speaks up. "Don't you think you ought to make sure the Tree Lord says we're guilty before you start raping people?"

Fabian kicks his dyitzu skin boots off. He doesn't even acknowledge Q except to unzip his old world jeans and pull out his semi-erect dick.

"Don't do it, Cid." My voice shakes as I speak.

Cid doesn't have to obey them. She's wearing infidel armor. The bullets would bounce off her. But then they'd know. They could go get the stone tipped arrows they use on the Icanitzu, or they could shoot her in the head.

Domina had been right. This takes something from you. You're never the same afterwards. You lose something.

They can't take that from Cid. She's too precious. Better to die.

She's stripping now, and true to her nature, does so without any sense of self-consciousness.

"Cid," I try to say something more, but nothing will come out.

The guards laugh. What the fuck is wrong with them? They have to know this is evil.

The pants of Cid's Icanitzu armor fall into a heap at her feet, and she steps out of them. Then, after tossing her top into one corner, she catches sight of Fabian's exposed member.

She smiles.

The fuck?

"Oh my," her voice is lusty, as if she's actually looking forward to her rape.

Her eyes open saucer wide, like some chick in an old world porno, ready to worship her man.

The hell is she doing? Her actions are so out of character, so revulsive . . .

It looks like some of the blood has gone out of the General, however. Had she known that? Had she anticipated that her desire would be unattractive to him? Please Cid. Please be smart enough to stop this.

I don't think I can witness this.

"Oh, you think you want it now," Fabian says, "but you won't in a minute." He nods to one of his chuckling white-cloaked men. "Open the bars."

"Yessir."

The soldier runs over to the pulley. Bells jingle as the bars rise. Fabian gets on his hands and knees, then crawls into the cell. For a second I think he won't fit.

The bottoms of the iron bars ruffle the overflowing mass of his red curls.

He squeezes through, the bells jingling as his caped back scrapes against the iron.

El Cid throws herself at him, not like an infidel, but like a woman throwing herself into her lover's arms. "Take me!" she begs.

He pushes her away and backhands her. The crack is loud, and I'm sure it would have done something to a normal woman.

But Cid lets out a pleased moan. "Hit me, Daddy! Punish me."

He backhands her across one cheek.

"Yes!" she shouts, offering up the other side of her face. "This one too."

He slaps her, hard, the smack echoing in the prison.

"More, sir. More!" Cid cries out. "Harder."

He rears back and slugs her. She tumbles backward, breaking her fall with her right arm slapping the ground.

"Yes!" she shouts.

"Shut up, cunt!" Fabian is fuming.

He falls atop her, his fists clenched. He slugs her again and again.

I can't let this happen. I rush forward, slamming myself against the bars. The bells jingle with my impact. I try to lift one, but the rough iron will not budge. I kick furiously at them.

Nothing.

"Hit me harder!" Cid continues. "More, please. Please."

Fabian's dick is floppy, completely unaroused. Cid's legs seem tiny. She's got them wrapped around his thick waist, but she can't cross her ankles to get into the safety position she showed me in training. Still, she's reaching up, as if to hug him. She's moving in all the right ways to make sure his punches aren't doing their worst. Her chin is tucked and her shoulders are hunched, so the blows don't seem to be rocking her — but they keep coming.

He pins her down with his left hand and brings his right down on her face like a hammer. Again and again and again.

"God, more!" Cid shouts in the throes of passion, her chin still firmly tucked. "You're so strong."

What the fuck is she doing? Is she going to make him beat her to death?

And that idea gives me hope. Better that than for her to know what it was like for me in Tintagel.

Fabian stops to catch his breath for a second, then he hits her, his fist cracking against her jaw. I hear her head rebound off the wooden floor.

I cover my mouth.

Oh, Cid.

But she doesn't lose consciousness.

"So strong!" she says, and sits up to reach for his

limp masculinity.

He slaps her down. "Fucking cunt!" he screeches.

Enraged beyond reason, Fabian begins another flurry. Cid is the toughest bitch I've ever seen in my life, but even so, this man outweighs her by the Devil knows how many pounds. Had she been able to actively defend herself, things might be going differently, but as it is . . .

"Beat me Daddy, beat me!" she cries.

Fabian's strikes have lost some of their venom. His flaccid dick is an impotent inch worm between his legs. I see him look back over his shoulder at his guards. He must be feeling shame. He must realize how weak he appears to be for not being able to knock out such a tiny girl.

God, is she going to pull this off?

His brow is slick with sweat. He sits back on his knees, panting hard. El Cid is up in a second, coming at him, kissing him, her hands running over his body as if she was his lover.

"Take me, Daddy!" she shouts.

"You sick . . . *bitch!*" Fabian's face is a brilliant red.

He's not going to be able to do it. He can't rape her. He must need to feel like he's in charge in order to get hard, but he has no control over Cid—and that must mortify him. She should be absolutely terrified of him. She should have been tricked into thinking that his actions toward her could cheapen her. But Cid isn't like that. Cid isn't human. She's a fucking infidel. She doesn't give a damn. She is that tiny voice inside our heads that screams at fate, that doesn't want to give up no matter how exhausting the trials, how dangerous the enemies, how hopeless the fight.

She can handle what destroyed me.

Cid reaches out to him. "Daddy, please! Please love me. I deserve your love. Don't I?"

Fabian half stands up, taking Cid with him, and dives forward. His head drives down into hers, and again I hear the crack of her skull as it impacts with the wood.

Jesus.

It's not going to work. Maybe against a slightly lesser man. She reaches up past his face with both hands, one palm up and the other palm down. Then, both hands gripping the man's cape, she maneuvers one arm around his head.

I'd not seen this hold before, but I realize it must be a choke. One forearm cuts across one corroded artery while her free hand tugs a part of Fabian's cape across the other—forming a vice around his neck.

A flurry of thoughts run through my mind. Will they shoot her for this? If Fabian wakes up, will he be too ashamed to do anything, or will he have her killed in a fit of revenge? How will this affect our trial?

"Cid!" Q yells a warning, clearly thinking similar thoughts.

But what does Q expect her to do? Do we want her to get raped just to increase our chances of survival?

The two white-cloaked guards can't tell what's going on, but they clearly understand, maybe from Fabian's body language or Q's shout, that something isn't right. Fabian's head is beet red, and it looks like he may not stay conscious for long.

He tries to stand up and press all of his substantial weight into her, but her leg snakes around his head, her choke still in place, and she wraps him up in an arm bar.

Break his arm, Cid. Just do it, we'll worry about the consequences later.

Fabian grunts loudly as he lifts her into the air, his arm and neck still caught in her ingenious hold. Then he rushes to the side of the cell and slams her into the wall.

Cid's arm comes loose just in time to slap the side of her cell in the perfect mimicry of a breakfall. Then she topples unconscious to the ground. But why? Why would she be unconscious? I didn't see her head get hit that time?

Fabian kicks her limp body. Will he be able to get hard now? Will he kill her if he can't?

"Fabian!" I shout, because a man like him shouldn't be allowed to hurt a girl like her.

Fabian looks at me, panting heavily, sweat weighing down his red curls. He's trying to look furious and disgusted instead of out of breath and impotent.

I grab the bars. "If you're looking to fuck the unwilling, I'm your John."

I hear Q chortle in the next room. The levity of his reaction assures me that Cid's okay, but I don't dare let a smile touch my face.

"Open the door!" Fabian yells, his blue eyes focused on me.

He looks almost relieved, though, and perhaps he's glad he has some way to save face.

The bars open to the jingling of the bells.

"No!" Cid yells, pretending to come to. "Don't leave me, Daddy. Don't fucking leave me!"

Fabian crawls ungracefully out. For a moment I wonder if Cid is going to hurt him, but she stays in character. She throws herself at the bars, reaching for him . . . her fingers just missing his holster.

I catch my breath.

Her face is fucked. One of her eyes is swollen shut and her nose is surely broken. Her lip is split open, she's cut in a couple of places, and I can see where blood matts her hair.

"Don't leave me!" she croons.

Fabian stumbles to his feet, off balance, his dick still bouncing about. He comes up to my cage. I realize that he really might rape me, like Melvin and Fellman had. He draws his pistol, thank God.

I turn and duck, trying to keep my head out of his line of fire.

He shoots, the blast deafening in the tight confines, the bullet splintering the wood next to me. His men are shouting madly over the ringing in my ears. I dare a peak back.

Cid is reaching through the bars. "Daddy!"

His men are grabbing him. "Sir! You can't kill him!" one cries. "The Tree Lord will have your head, sir."

Fabian grabs his boots, his member still exposed, and storms out. I hear his feet slapping against the wooden stairs. His two men stand there, sharing a look. Then they follow after their leader.

"Cid!" I call, and I reach out to her.

She stands, victorious—nude but inviolate. Blood is pouring down from her nose and from a cut under her swollen-shut eye. It runs off the point of her tiny chin.

"Are you okay, Cid?" I ask.

She shrugs her shoulders. "I'm fine." Her voice sounds almost as nasal as Fabian's.

She reaches one hand up to her face, and I hear the crunching of cartilage as she sets her own broken nose.

"I'm fine," she repeats.

I hear a series of bootsteps on the stairs.

Nothing good ever comes from that noise.

I begin moving my arms and legs, limbering them up for whatever damnable confrontation awaits us.

Amirani enters the room, his slender shoulders and black cape infinitely preferable to the broad, green-caped monstrosity that had come through that same archway earlier.

I let out a relieved sigh.

My neck pops as I stretch it. My muscles scream as I climb to my feet, but I welcome their discomfort.

Amirani's face is the typical expressionless infidel mask, so I have no idea whether the news is going to be bad or good . . . until he catches sight of Cid, her bloody face, and her swollen-shut eye.

"Jesus," he breathes. "Are you okay?"

She grins. "You can't tell I'm winking at you?"

My heart swells a little with pride for my leader, and I allow myself to smile with her. She is an unbelievably tough bitch.

All five of us—myself, Aiden, Q, Neb and the battered Cid—step up to the bars. Of the prisoners, only Durgan remains at the back of his cage. He doesn't fool me, though, that fucker is eavesdropping.

"The hearing has been set," Amirani says, "we've got tonight to prepare you."

I point to Durgan. "He can overhear us."

Amirani nods. "Yes, but he won't be joining us on the first day. Tertiary witnesses are usually called on day two—assuming we make it that far."

Neb, ghost pale, his body clearly wrecked from the run, asks, "What are our chances?"

"Of making it past day two?" Amirani frowns thoughtfully. "Pretty good."

"Why?" Cid asks.

"Not because of the strength of our case," Amirani says sardonically. "The drama of a trial will help people forget about the attacks." He turns around, meeting all of our eyes. "We've got a two-part plan. First, we discredit Keith and show that Durgan here is a plant for our enemies. After that comes the hard part. We have to convince the crowd you deserve mercy for a crime that, quite frankly, we're guilty of." He glances at Aiden. "Everyone with me?"

We nod in unison, even my son.

He's a good kid. Well, not technically, but—

Q clears his throat. "What about this infused man, Callodax? His army? Are we in any danger from them while the trial goes on?"

Amirani takes in a breath. "Very possibly. As for who they are, I've verified that you were right about them being Carrion born, Igraine's people specifically. They've made some kind of deal with the infused. Just so you know, Keith's been back to Dendra twice since you left for Soulfall. How the infused managed to get such a hold over Keith's men, and over the Carrion born so quickly, I don't know. I've verified that the infused is controlling the devils, using an Icanitzu Lord to grant him that authority."

I hear Q hit the wall, I assume in frustration.

Amirani turns to me. "I think Callodax might view his human army as less expendable than his demons, and by having the demons take all the bullets, his men will have an easier go of it in a final assault. His devil attacks have badly depleted Dendra's ammunition."

"And this Varadoolyn?" I ask. "Brother Durgan over here," I point at the wight, who, like the bastard he is, nods back to me politely, "is said to be serving an Archdevil by that name."

Amirani shakes his head. "That is the line Durgan gave to his interrogators, but it's almost certainly a lie. However, Dendra is pretty proud of having 'extracted' that information from him, so they're not likely to doubt it. The real devil out there is the infused, and that's the leverage we're going to use to kick Keith's ass out of this city."

I lean against the bars. "Now you're talking."

"I took one of the treemen scouting with me. Now this treeman *hates* infidels, but he's honest, so he'll make a very convincing witness. Together, he and I were able to eavesdrop on the infused while he was speaking with an Icanitzu. Callodax was having trouble convincing the entire murder of Icanitzu and dezendyitzu to keep the attacks up. The treeman's testimony, because he hates us so much, should be enough to kick Keith and his boys out of Dendra. Then we'll only have the Accuser to deal with."

I'm starting to think we might have a real shot at this.

"Getting Keith out is only the first part," Amirani goes on. "You'll still have to beat the charges of abetting a wight. Your Accuser, think of him as the prosecuting attorney, was an actual attorney in the old world, so we'll be at a disadvantage sophistically speaking."

I raise my hand slowly, but even so, my back is tight enough that I nearly pull a muscle.

"Yeah, Cris?"

"I thought infidels were supposed to be really good at arguing?" I ask.

He shrugs. "We're a bit too occupied with finding the truth to be perfect in this context. The Tree Lord is our jury, judge, and of course, executioner, and his taste in argumentation is a little . . . unrefined."

I shrug. "I've always been more style than substance."

Cid frowns. "Be careful, Cris. Make sure you don't make the Tree Lord doubt your honesty."

"That's a good point," Amirani says. "Now our intellectual honesty is pretty shot anyway, on account of our earlier lie." He looks at me. "I'd ask you not do that again, by the way."

"How are they sure we lied?" I ask. "If Keith and his boys tattled on us to the Tree Lord, can't we just say they made the whole thing up?"

Amirani frowns. "Well, for one, Aiden's state is proof against us. But even before you returned, I was caught. The actual, uh, tattler, was a girl named Ghela. She witnessed your lie about us having the Tree Lord's blessing. She didn't actually know we were lying when she heard it, which made her testimony against me pretty damning. There's a lot of things that bother the Tree Lord, but none so much as 'taking his name in vain.' Your best bet is to point out that you only brought a wight into the city because of the extenuating circumstances of an attack. You would have liked to have asked the Lord for permission, but the time required would have been cost prohibitive."

"What's that mean?" Aiden asks. "Cost prohibitive?"

Man, he's actually paying attention.

"It means it would have taken too long," Amirani answers, his eyes narrowing as he regards my son. "Now, on your first time through Dendra, when Aiden was on edge, you were clearly in the wrong." He turns toward Cid. "Our hope is to make ourselves as likable as possible to the crowd. Now, I've seen the people of Dendra sway the Tree Lord before. He pretends to be aloof, but in his heart, he wants to be loved by his people. We need to set up an environment where the Tree Lord can make some grand sweeping gesture of mercy." He looks again to Aiden. "Avoiding the fall will be a longshot for most of us, but for you, little Aiden . . . well, we need a straight-up miracle for you. When you're being questioned, you're going to have to sell how good a person you are. No matter your personal beliefs, no matter how you feel about your father and the others, your own survival depends on Dendra thinking you're good."

Aiden nods. "I'll do my best."

Amirani doesn't trust Aiden, clearly. Maybe he shouldn't. Maybe I'm an idiot for believing there is a spark of good left in my boy.

Maybe the right thing really is to toss my son into

the endless fog.

"For all of us, delay is best." Amirani smiles. "Alright, I'll be stopping by each of your cages to coach you personally for the trial. Save any questions you have until then." He looks pointedly at Durgan.

So now he's going to tell us the shit he doesn't want Durgan to overhear.

He moves over to Aiden's cage. Their conversation is soft enough that I can't hear it.

I'm overwhelmed with the need to be free. With the need to run on my beyond-sore muscles. I'm filled with a flight urge so strong it's all I can do to prevent myself from charging headlong toward the bars.

Instead I sit down.

After being imprisoned by Igraine, holing up in the safe house, and finally being imprisoned here, I'm starting to feel like I'll be trapped forever.

My deeper worry, that fear that I might actually be in the wrong, springs up again. As a normal man, I was free to think I was in the right simply because I was me. As an infidel, shit gets a bit more complicated.

I'm going to have to let that go. Time enough to be an infidel later. Right now, I need to survive. Right now, I need to believe in myself. Believe that I'm doing the right thing. Believe that I and my son are worth saving.

VIII

This morning there are a great many men coming down our stairs. I wish they'd never make it to the bottom step and that this moment would be frozen in time. Then I might not ever have to face my fate, or watch my son face his.

Dendra's wicker-helmed soldiers come marching in, two by two.

Amirani is there, but so is Fabian. They are side by side, the twin pillars of Dendra's military community. I realize now just how divisive this trial might be, as it will pit the two most influential warriors of this city against each other. Amirani, I know, will be content to wage this war using only the laws of Dendra. Fabian, on the other hand—who knew what that fucker would do.

I don't know what it says about a man when he can't get it up in the face of consent.

The pillars of the community of Dendra are such different figures, the slender infidel dressed in black dwarfed by the menacing green-cloaked and red-bearded hulk towering beside him.

Amirani's visage is the model of infidel stoicism, giving nothing away.

Fabian, however, is pissed off, and his white-knuckled fists clench when he sees Cid. She seems a shit ton better, at least. Other than around her eye, the swelling has almost completely died away, though purple bruises and dried blood still mark her face. Infidels heal fast.

"Ready your weapons," Fabian orders.

His treemen raise their bows and arrows.

He grins through his red beard. "Now open the cages."

The two white-cloaked men he'd brought with him during his attempted rape move to the chains. Bells jingle as the mobile bars of each cage rise. I stretch and begin to crawl through. It's a struggle for Neb and I, but Cid and Q slip out like the infidel bastards they are.

Of course, it's no trouble at all for my son. He's always been a squirrely little fucker, and undeath hasn't changed that.

Josh won't meet my eyes. That's not a good sign.

"Two guards per prisoner," Fabian intones. "I'll help with the bitch."

He walks over and grabs Cid's arm with enough force to nearly knock her off her feet.

"I like your grip," Cid gushes.

Fabian readies a backhand.

"Stop." Amirani's cool voice cuts through the air. "She's not been found guilty yet, Fabian. You'd not want to beat an innocent woman."

A few of the treemen snicker, though I don't see a damn thing funny about this.

"Lead them up," Fabian orders.

Josh takes me by one arm, and some guard I don't recognize seizes me by the other.

Together, we travel up the dark, spiral staircase.

Our heavy footsteps echo, meshing together oddly with the staccato beat of our captors' as we go. We emerge onto the main landing of the Wicker Tree.

Josh points through a gap in the vines to the vast expanse of Dendra. "That, that's the Tree Lord's tree. The Prima Tree. Court is held on a platform near the bottom. You can't see it from here, but when we get out on the bridges, you will."

"And what's that?" I point through another gap, out across the breadth of the chamber to where a bridge, not one of these shit bridges, but an actual wooden planked bridge, runs in nearly a straight line from tree to tree."

He grimaces. "The longbridge. Leads to the Safe Tree."

I nod. "Where your family will be if I need to rescue them."

The other guard's grip becomes tighter, but Josh's loosens.

"Yes," he says.

I breathe in the air, and I can practically feel the sappy scent in the back of my throat.

Fabian leads us with Cid on his arm. She's clinging to him, switching her hips, walking along as if she's his girlfriend, not his prisoner. I smile. That girl knows how to piss people off.

It's the little things in life.

As a group, we head to the bridges. Neb is slowing us up. I was feeling pretty limber, all things considered, but the former Nazi is not having a good time of it. He's hobbling more than walking, and his guards are pestering him to go faster.

That's okay, I have no particular wish to get to the hearing on time.

We've got this. We just have to follow Amirani's plan. Step one, kick out Keith. Step two, beat the charges . . . that is, assuming Callodax doesn't attack us in the middle of the damn trial and slaughter us all.

Fabian, Cid, and one of the white-cloaked guards step onto the bridge we'll take. It's not worth it, but I'm hoping Cid would toss that fucker into the mists.

The vines still hang thick on the branches of the Wicker Tree, but there are hints of the enormity that is Dendra through their gaps. Some of those gaps, lined with blackened and charred plant matter, were clearly made by dyitzu fireballs.

They take Q next, then Aiden.

They're a little rough with my son, but he ignores it well.

"We're up," Josh tells me.

We walk onto the bridge. Amirani is right behind us, staying close.

We clear the vines and are exposed to the chamber's tremendous hellscape. The mists are low, and I can see all of the oversized trees in their splendor and glory. The brown dressed Dendran citizens are out, lining the walkways, landings and branches which overlook our path. I guess we're big news.

Amirani whispers from behind me. "Remember when I told you about the scouting I did yesterday, and my friend?"

I don't look back at him, but both of my guards do.

"Yes," I say.

"The witness of the Icanitzu meeting died last night. He fell."

Fuck.

"They'll believe you, though, won't they?" I ask.

Amirani doesn't answer. He doesn't have to. I'm the one who made him a liar.

Well so much for step one.

A leaf falls from the tree ahead, sailing this way and that in the air as it descends. I realize the leaf is dangerous. It is the size of a person, and while it might not take out a bridge, it could certainly shake one.

Fortunately, this leaf only touches another branch as it makes its way down.

Our witness died? Really? We couldn't be *that* unlucky, but how could Callodax even know they needed to kill the scout? Keith must have found out somehow.

A young girl, maybe six, is high on a platform by a root at a sap tapping station. She waves at us, perhaps too young to understand who we are and what we've done. Others peek at me from within wicker houses as we pass alongside the Storage Tree.

I look longingly at one of the Storage Tree's entrances. My pack is in there, and I feel naked without it.

The landing they call the square is the most stable of any I've seen so far. Its burnished planks are nailed together, supported by a complex of latticework and two of the Prima Tree's huge branches. I'd bet money Amirani supervised building this thing.

The platform joins with its tree where a huge cut had been made into the trunk. The indention looks for all the world as if Paul Bunyan had made it with an axe swing. Inside the epically-sized indention, a chair sits at the back edge of the cut. As far as chairs go, the high back and arm rests make it look suspiciously throne-like.

There's a flimsy wooden cage, maybe ten feet wide, on the right side of the platform. Its door is open, and I have a sinking feeling that we're going to be put in it.

The crowd of Dendrans is massive. They mill about in their dyitzu skin smocks and wicker headwear. A few young souls move impatiently amongst them, some climbing like monkeys along vines and branches. One parent is shouting as his child descends from some latticework. The groups of people we passed earlier in our journey are slowly filtering in behind us, bottlenecked at the bridges. They move in small groups, three at a time, from the surrounding trees.

"You're famous now," one guard says. "The Tree Lord's even got them setting up extra bridges for you."

The extra bridges he's referring to are quite brilliantly designed. They attach trios of vines to both ends of a gap using what I'm guessing is processed spider silk. The thickest vine makes the floor of the bridge while the other two act as guard rails. It doesn't seem to be the safest structure, but apparently it'll do in a pinch.

Pairs of Dendrans toss the silk-ended vines across the gaps. As I watch, one man gets his hand caught in the sticky silk. I chuckle a little when he can't get the substance off. I figure he's shit out of luck, but another treeman douses his hand with a ready water bucket, and that loosens the adhesive enough to where he can free himself.

The Dendran citizens begin crossing those bridges in groups of three, but we're forced along one of the permanent bridges.

The guards clear a path for us, and we make our way across the fifty-yard expanse of planks, nails and vines of the Prima Tree's platform.

Fabian stops and whispers into a young woman's ear. She's a stocky brunette whose hair is braided up like someone from a renaissance fair. She kisses him. Nasty. What kind of woman would be with a thing like Fabian?

I think about it more deeply.

That poor girl.

As I expected, we are ushered into the cage. Its bars are made of sticks and rope. It wouldn't make a good long term prison, but they have enough guards to make up for it. Hey, at least we'll have a good view.

There is a raised stage, maybe twenty feet from the king, which has four guards around it. That's got to be the witness stand.

The buzz around us dies down after we're locked in the cage. There's barely enough space for all of us in here. I'm guessing they usually try one person at a time.

The hum of conversation makes a comeback, though, increasing steadily as more people file in.

When it's loud enough, I dare to pass on Amirani's information. "Amirani just told me his witness died. We're not going to be able to get rid of Keith."

Cid and Q don't react at all. Is it possible they'd known already? Neb, however, is troubled.

I put my hand on Aiden's shoulder. His black eyes remain fixed on the crowd, his face calm and determined.

"We're going to be okay, son," I tell him.

He shakes his head. "Don't lie to me."

The lovely redhead who'd fed me before moves in and out of the leaf shadows which dapple the trunk on the left side of the Tree Lord's throne. She might be coming this way. Then I catch sight of Keith. He's regained his composure, but I bet that's a façade. Instinctively I want to poke at him, to piss him off, to see just how thin that layer of sanity is.

Many of the onlookers are staring at us, a few at me. They don't meet my eyes. People love to watch train wrecks, and I'm sure they'd be happy to watch us take the fall.

I lean against the side of my wooden cage. The ropes creak under my weight. I smell something sweet, a sappy scent I remember. Out of the corner of my eye I see her red hair. She looks different in the light, but she's still absolutely gorgeous. There's an edge to her I'd not noticed in the darkness. A cruelness, perhaps.

"Hi," I say softly.

She does not respond with words but inclines her head, which makes sense. Who in their right mind would want to be seen talking to me?

The hum of conversation nearly stops, but a single oblivious onlooker keeps on, his voice made more annoying by a New Jersey accent. Some people hush him, and though he tries to speak again, the continued insistence of the crowd silences him.

A thin man, clad in a green, gold-trimmed robe, steps out of an opening in the Prima Tree's Paul Bunyan axe wound.

"That's him, the Tree Lord," the redhead whispers. "He lives in the chambers above. There are charges of infidel fire which Amirani set in the roots. If devils ever attack his tree, he can retreat into his safe rooms above and set off the explosions, sending the Prima Tree falling into the mists."

"That sounds appealing," I quip.

"That way he can stay safe in the caverns above while the rest of us are slaughtered," she says.

It seems I've made a friend.

"It's a safe setup," I say.

"He never has to worry about falling into the mists," she says. "He never has to walk the bridges or fight the devils. You see that counterweight system over there?"

Her nod is slight, so it takes me a minute to spot what she's talking about. But in the branches beyond the crowd, I see huge, cubic stone weights—perhaps ten feet wide—held up by a system of chains and pulleys.

"I see them."

She sneers. "Amirani had to finish them before the Tree Lord would let him bolster our defenses. Do you know what they do?"

"I don't."

"They bring up bloodwater barrels. That bastard is more concerned with getting drunk than our survival."

This clearly pisses her off, but at the moment, I feel like I wouldn't mind a gig like the Tree Lord's. It's certainly not the worst way to ride out damnation.

The Tree Lord looks up as he comes down a set of carved out wooden stairs. I shit you not, he seems exactly like a green robed Jesus. Not the first century Palestinian Jew of antiquity, but the blue eyed, light brown-haired, barely smiling Jesus whose face was a staple of renaissance art.

"God damn," I breathe.

"What?" she asks.

"I swear, every time Jesus sits in judgement of me, my life gets just a little bit worse."

She snickers.

Even the Tree Lord's mannerisms are suitably Christ-like. He touches people, smiling as he moves through the crowd, a look of pure love on his face.

He ascends to his throne.

The murmuring crowd forms a half moon around

the throne and the stage. They remain hushed as they shuffle — perhaps awaiting a proclamation from the Tree Lord.

I see Fabian there, at the edge of the crowd, his green cape slung over one shoulder. Amirani stays near us, perhaps making some show of solidarity.

Amirani said we had a good shot to make it to day two, right? But that was *before* we lost our scout.

I'm going to die.

The thought of the next Hell fills me with horror. My hands are shaking.

On Earth, when the afterlife was some half-believed dream, a man could make peace with death. You can't make your peace with death here because it marks an irrevocable downward step into the abyss of damnation. Every level lower is worse, and you can never come back up. It's like losing a limb in the old world. You'll never get it back. You'll always be less than you were.

Without warning, the idea of the infinite abyss below fills me with vertigo. I'm highly aware of how thin the platform I'm standing on is. Underneath my feet, mists await. The ground feels unstable, as if the weight of all these people is causing it to shake.

I turn to Cid. I want nothing more than to hold her hand, to feel her power, to rest my fate in the strength of her will.

But I can't show weakness before this crowd. And I

can't show the redhead that my heart belongs to another because I need her to love me.

The Tree Lord sits. "For three days the devils attacked us, and for three days they were repelled. Why? Why did they attack? Did they sense weakness amongst us? Or did strangers bring sin into Dendra?"

The crowd jeers and the Tree Lord smiles his Jesus smile.

I have the sudden urge to nail that fucker up on a cross.

He holds up his hand and, after a moment, the jeering stops. "Please, bring the wight. Let us sit in judgement of the creature."

IX

The door to our cage swivels open.

Aiden turns to me, terror in his inhumanly pale face, his black eyes wide.

"I love you, son," I tell him.

The arms of the guards reach in and grab my boy. They drag him away, and I feel my heart going with him.

My hand instinctively reaches for Cid's, but she's as still as stone.

I look to Q, who is similarly stoic. It's Neb who meets my gaze, not because he's the only one who can feel my sorrow, but because he's the only one poorly trained enough to show emotion.

And for that, I am *so* grateful. Necromancer and

Nazi he may be, but he's still human, and his support gives me something.

I turn to the redhead. Her eyes are on some distant tree—the Safe Tree, I believe. From the conversation I overheard with Josh, I know that's where they move children and non-combatants in times of assault. Maybe she's got a loved one in there.

The jeers come again as they drag my boy to the stand.

The crowd recoils as Aiden walks up the steps. It's as if Aiden's elevation to the stage repulses them. My son seems so defiant, so vulnerable. His tattered dyitzu skin shirt hangs off his stick-like torso. His hair, so blond, so fair, is still darker than his marble white skin.

I feel a love in my heart which is mixed with terror and pride.

I made you.

I'm sorry, son. I didn't make you strong enough for this, but I made you as strong as I could.

"Creature," the Tree Lord addresses my son, "you entered our city on two occasions. Once, as a leper, and again as a wight. Tell me, what is it that wights want most in Hell?"

The redhead shifts. "That's the same question he asked Durgan when he was up here," she whispers.

Aiden raises his chin. "I don't know."

"That's not what Durgan said," she informs me. "He said he lived to watch us suffer."

My son better lie his little wight ass off.

"Do you want to watch us suffer?" the Tree Lord asks.

"No," Aiden says, shaking his head.

"You're lying."

Aiden looks at his feet.

"We've heard from another of your kind," the Tree Lord booms, speaking now as much to the gathered crowd as to Aiden. "We know you desire to torture us. We know that your mind is filled with the Devil's thoughts. We know."

The crowd murmurs in agreement.

"We know!" the Tree Lord proclaims, raising his hands to the delight of the onlookers.

Aiden shakes his head again. "I don't!" he shouts. "I didn't choose to be a wight. My mother made me one. She fed me wightdust because she was in love with some demon. But I'm not. I don't love the Devil. I love my father."

Is he acting?

So many people take in a breath that the crowd sounds like a hungry fire sucking in oxygen. My son bolts, dark tears streaming from his eyes, his legs propelling him toward the side of the stage nearest me. The guards lunge forward to stop him even as the crowd retreats. The treemen catch him, but Aiden doesn't struggle. Instead he cries in their arms, his hands reaching out to me.

His high voice cries out, "Cris! Save me."

His plea tugs at me and I'm pulled by it into the wooden bars. The ropes creak with the force of my weight.

Now the crowd is reacting to him differently. They step forward, as if no longer disgusted.

The guards climb up onto the stand, one of them carrying Aiden. They put him down roughly, facing him toward the Tree Lord.

"Answer the question." The Tree Lord is unfazed. "What do wights want?"

"I told you," Aiden whines, "I don't know. I just know what *I* want. I want to be with my father. I want to kill devils. They made me drink the dust. I didn't want it."

People mutter amongst themselves.

A sparrow flies over us. Come on, little bird, you know you want to shit on the Tree Lord.

It doesn't.

Traitor.

"Why did you enter our city?" the Tree Lord asks.

Aiden raises his chin again. "I was barely conscious the first time. We had to make it to the Erebus quickly. They wanted to save me, to stop me from becoming this. We almost made it . . . but Dad said we were just a little late."

"And the second?" the Tree Lord asks.

"We were being chased by Keith's people. They

were trying to kill us, so we ran. They drove us and a horde of creatures into you."

Everyone looks at Keith.

I grin. My son may be doomed, but he's kicking ass up there. I wonder how much of it is Amirani's coaching.

A man wearing a white T-shirt approaches the stage. "If you wouldn't mind, sir, I'd like to ask a couple of questions."

"You are the Accuser, that is your right," the Tree Lord agrees.

"Do you feel any different now that you're a wight?" the Accuser asks.

Aiden shifts from foot to foot. "I don't get tired. It's harder to feel things sometimes. It's like my feelings come to me through some fog. But I still feel. It's like my soul is far away."

The Accuser waits for the crowd to quiet. "Has it gotten any farther away in the time that you've been a wight?"

Aiden shakes his head. "No, it's like the fog is clearing, and I'm more and more me."

I've no idea if these statements are true, but I hope like hell they are.

"So you like other children?" the Accuser asks.

Cid shifts beside me.

Aiden nods slowly.

The Accuser motions to his right.

A man comes out, an infant in his arms.

Aiden is stone faced.

I hear Q mutter under his breath.

"What?" I whisper. "What's going on?"

El Cid's lips barely move as she answers me. "Could your son, before he was a wight, make no reaction as a child was tortured in front of him?"

I think about this. "I don't know."

And that's the truth. His formative years happened under Myla's influence. I'd not known him since he was four.

The infant laughs as the Accuser lifts it high into the air. The man turns quickly around so as to make the baby seem to fly.

The infant gurgles in delight.

Oh, that's what Q had told me. To a wight, a child laughing is like a child crying.

Aiden remains stone faced.

The Accuser walks up the steps of the stand and holds the baby up to Aiden.

The crowd again sucks in a breath, probably fearing for the child's life.

Aiden twitches. Then, as the infant giggles, Aiden turns his head away.

"This wight is an excellent liar," the Accuser says. "See how he's disgusted by little Ethan? I'm not surprised. Now I won't say for certain that he didn't fool the infidels. It's possible, I suppose, they really do believe this thing before us is good. I don't think so, but they might. Even so, they should know better, and that doesn't make their breaking the law any more acceptable."

He takes the baby down the steps.

Aiden is looking at his feet again.

Damn. That did not go well.

"I'm satisfied," the Tree Lord says. "Amirani, do you have any questions you'd like to add?"

I'm not sure how he's going to undo that, but he's an infidel. I'm sure he'll think of something.

Amirani shakes his head. "No, Tree Lord. I have nothing to add."

Fuck. This had better be like one of those movies where the lawyer is silent for the whole trial and then drops a motherfucking truth bomb to save the day at the end.

"Then let's bring out the Nazi," the Tree Lord says.

Nebuchadnezzar shares a nod with my son as they pass each other in the cage's doorway. Two treemen flank him as he strides toward the stage, his boots clopping loudly on the wooden floor. The crowd doesn't seem to know what to think of him, which is odd. For Neb's part, he doesn't appear to care about the crowd at all.

He mounts the steps quickly and stands, legs spread shoulder width, his chin raised. He looked half-dead when they dragged us here, but all this hate seems to have given him a second wind.

"You don't seem very respectful of the proceedings," the Tree Lord notes.

Nebuchadnezzar snorts. "This is hardly

Nuremberg."

Q quickly covers his mouth. The crowd buzzes.

"A death sentence here is just as fatal," the Tree Lord shoots back.

"If I wanted to avoid your justice, I could," Nebuchadnezzar says. "I'd tell you how I didn't dare cross the infidels, and that I led them to Soulfall against my will or my better judgement, and you'd forgive me."

"You went to Soulfall?" the Tree Lord asks.

"Yes," Neb answers.

Some in the crowd stir, but I'm betting most people don't know what that place is.

The Tree Lord shifts in his throne. "You said 'if.'"

Nebuchadnezzar grimaces. "I'll not tell you those things."

"Then why did you, other than the fact you are a Nazi, help smuggle a wight into my city?"

"I protest," he says, and for just that moment I hear the German accent in his voice. "I am damned, but I am no Nazi."

I'm really starting to like this guy. Fuck me for it, but I am.

"Oh?" The Tree Lord smirks. "Are you an infidel now?"

Neb cocks his head to one side. "I'm trying to be, my Lord."

"The guilt starting to get ya?" The Tree Lord still seems amused.

"Yes," Neb says flatly.

The Tree Lord's face goes grim, and he sits up straight before leaning forward. "Why did you bring a wight into my city? Twice!"

"The second time was clearly understandable," Neb says, pointing to Keith. "You should put him on trial for that—"

The Accuser breaks in. "You might as well accuse Ethan! How can you hold someone else responsible?"

Neb cocks his head again. "I certainly shall accuse the babe, the second Ethan grows up, gets an army, and herds me here against my will."

The crowd fucking loves that. They burst into jeers. One of the children starts to cry. The Tree Lord raises his hands, silencing the entire crowd except the child.

"But the first time—" the necromancer begins.

"Now wait just a second," the Accuser breaks in.

"Why not," Neb says. "It's your damn trial. Why would you care what I have to say?"

The Tree Lord raises his hands again to silence the hoots and hollers, clearly exasperated. "Please, continue to answer *my* question."

Neb grins at the Accuser. Then his face becomes serious. "I don't really follow the infidels. I follow Cris. We all wanted a parent who loved us more than anything. Who would protect us. If my father had been like that, maybe I wouldn't have become a Nazi, I don't know. But Cris is that kind of parent. His son was stolen from him, taken to the darkened city of Maylay Beighlay. The boy was lost by anyone's reckoning. Anyone but Cris'. He marched into that city and killed an Archdevil. I'm thinking you already owe him for that. Then he dragged his half dead son out of there. Are any of you fathers? We're all children.

"When the infidels came to my home, I had intended to send them away. I couldn't, not when Cris asked me to go. I follow him because I don't want to be what I am. I don't want to be a Nazi. I think his will is enough, enough to cancel out the wight in his son. It's been enough so far. I know you doubt Aiden's intentions, and to tell you the truth, so do the infidels. But you know infidels; they have to study everything. The plan was to slay Aiden at the first sign of his turning."

The Accuser stands up. "May I, now?"

The Tree Lord sighs. "Go ahead."

"I just showed that the wight was evil. As soon as he was out of your reach, as soon as you had a moment of weakness, that wight would have escaped. He would have begun killing."

Neb frowns. "I thought as you did. Even I, a necromancer, wanted the boy killed. The two circumstances you speak of, however, where the boy was out of our reach, and when we were incapacitated . . . well they've both happened, multiple times—both before and after we had him in our custody. As for the rationale behind *why* the boy behaves morally, you'll have to ask someone else."

"You don't deny bringing a wight into our city?" the Tree Lord asks.

"I was complicit with bringing a leper into your city. At that point, he wasn't yet a wight. Keith's the one who brought a full on wight in."

The Tree Lord pops his tongue on the roof of his mouth. "Leper or wight, the sentence is the fall." He points down.

Neb shrugs. "I really couldn't give two shits what a man like you wants to do to me."

Damn it, Neb!

The Tree Lord leaps to his feet. "You, who slaughtered innocents by the millions, attack my character?"

Neb nods. "I'm sure you know what Fabian does to your prisoners. Even at my worst, I would never have allowed that."

There is another silence, and this time it affects even the child. They know. This whole damn town knows. But no one looks at Fabian. Not a damn one of them. Oh God they must want to, but they just don't dare.

Fabian speaks up. "We've heard enough of this, my Lord."

The Tree Lord motions to Amirani. "Anything you're curious about?"

Amirani shakes his head.

Neb doesn't wait for a dismissal, but instead marches down the stairs, his grey overcoat swirling about his ankles. His guards have to jog to keep up with him as he heads to our cage.

"Bring the leader up next," the Tree Lord orders.

Cid seems so tiny on the stage. She crosses her arms beneath her small breasts. From this distance I can barely tell that she'd been beaten the day before. Only the red and purple discolorations on her face and right eye give any hint of her trauma.

"You seem to have taken some damage in your journey," the Tree Lord remarks.

She shrugs. "A little from that, Lord. A little of it was from Fabian trying to work himself up to an erection."

The crowd is eerily silent.

Cid turns to Fabian's woman. "Don't worry, miss, he failed. You aren't a cuckold. I must not have been attractive enough."

The woman's face, a mask of anger after Cid's erection comment, breaks down into despair as she lets out a choked sob. Cid knows how to kick a person verbally.

Cid's arms fall to her sides. "He'll beat you tonight, you know that, don't you?"

The Tree Lord clears his throat. "If you are to make

such accusations—"

Cid raises a hand, and for some unearthly reason, the Tree Lord stops speaking. She steps to the edge of the platform, then glares down toward Fabian even as she continues speaking to his wife. "Poor girl, he'll beat you for what I said. He'll have some excuse, but you'll know it's because of me. You'll know I unmanned him, and that you have to take the beating for it."

Fabian turns red.

Finally, the crowd reacts, breaking out into a buzz of boos and worried murmurs.

Cid returns her attention to the Tree Lord. "You ought not allow that beating to happen, Lord. If she comes to you, will you offer her your soldiers' protection?"

"There's no need for that," the Tree Lord says. "No need at all. I trust Fabian."

Cid shrugs. "If I were a betting girl, I'd say Fabian already beat her after his attempt to rape me. Why not have her take off her shirt to show the bruises."

Will the Tree Lord allow this? Probably not.

"The bruises are from a fall," Fabian's woman says quickly in his defense, but that's probably the worst defense I've ever heard in my life.

Just like that, the idea that Fabian might not be some insane woman-beating-psycho-rapist was untenable.

Fabian is fuming, his hate-filled eyes focused on his

wife—only beating her for what she said wouldn't help him much now.

Cid addresses the Tree Lord, "The monsters I keep don't beat defenseless women."

Amirani steps back quickly, and Neb stiffens. I think she may have just condemned us to the fall. Is everyone going to pick a fight with the Tree Lord?

"That will be a separate trial, at a separate time." Any hint of the Tree Lord's Jesus-like expression of calm is gone. "You will answer my questions."

Cid adjusts her stance so that she's facing the Tree Lord. She clasps her hands behind her back and nods her assent. "I shall answer."

"You took a wight into this city?" he asks.

"As has been previously said, I did not. We were herded into the city by Keith's soldiers. We are guilty of smuggling a leper through your city in hopes of reclaiming his soul. We did not consult you, and we are guilty of breaking that law. It is our request that you grant us clemency since it was an errand of mercy."

"I'm running short on mercy," the Tree Lord booms.

Cid smirks. "I can imagine. After forgiving Fabian, it seems like you'd be running a little low."

Again the crowd breaks into angry muttering—but the anger is starting to find a better focal point. Fabian gives a few furtive looks to his neighbors.

"Why did you not kill the wight?" the Tree Lord

yells. "Infidels are not supposed to spare devils."

"Because it's not over," Cid says.

Now every eye is on her, including mine. For just a moment, I feel something stir deep inside me. Hope.

No. Fuck hope. Fuck her. Hope's destroyed me. Every sacrifice I make, every effort, every damn step I've taken toward hope has left me lower. I slayed a God damn Archdevil to rescue my son, and did I get him back? No. I got a godforsaken leper. And then I carried him across Hell to face Soulfall, and I won, and did I get my son back? No. Hell gave me a wight. But not a normal wight, a wight with just enough humanity for there to be something left to lose.

But I know what happens next. That last part of him will be ripped away.

There is no hope in Hell.

There is no hope. Cid is lying to manipulate the Tree Lord, and there is no chance that my son can be restored.

"What's not over?" the Tree Lord is asking.

"The boy," Cid says. "He's not lost. There is a way, and Nebuchadnezzar can confirm this, that even a full-blooded wight can be restored. Only, so far, there has been no wight willing to try it. This could be the one exception. I couldn't kill the wight because, right now, that's only the body of a wight. The soul is still the soul of a little boy, and as an infidel, I have no right to slay him. Now believe me, if I had the first inclination that he was turning the rest of the way, I would have destroyed him." She turns to Fabian. "Like I will destroy you for what you tried to do to me."

This pushes him over the edge. "You? You destroy me? You're about to be back in my prison, missy."

El Cid shakes her head and points to the Tree Lord. "In *his* prison. And if you try to rape me again, then you will assure that I don't fall, but that you do. Everyone knows what you do."

The Tree Lord clenches the armrests of his throne and pushes himself to his feet. "I said that is for another day. We have just survived a siege, El Cid, and you walk in here destabilizing my forces . . ."

Cid shrugs. "Give me a gun, I'll defend your city. Give me my team, I'll go out and clear away your enemies."

"You pled guilty to the charges," the Accuser says. "The rest is you using your infidel training to confuse the issue. This case is, however, black and white. You are guilty."

El Cid looks at him. "Yes. I'm not lying. I'm not going to say I didn't break the law. I'm asking the Tree Lord if the law needs to be changed because it doesn't appear to be just in this circumstance."

"Everyone has excuses," the Accuser says. "Everyone can justify why they did their crime. The law is black and white so that people like you will know that if they do a thing, they will face the consequences."

"I suppose," El Cid says. "That line of reasoning would have been a great excuse. It would've allowed me to give up on a soul that is not yet lost. It would let me murder a child."

God, Cid kicks ass.

The Accuser purses his lips. "A wight, you mean. It would let you *murder* a wight. Which is your job, isn't it? As an infidel?"

"My job is to help human souls."

"By putting our lives in danger?" he shouts. "You brought this monster among us, hoping against hope that you're right about him. But you know you're wrong. And here you are, a wight at your side, gambling our lives on your hunch!"

She turns to him. "I had no intention of coming here. I was driven by—"

"Yes, yes, I know!" the Accuser breaks in. "Convenient of you to defend that infraction! But you brought the leper here, risking our city, of your own free will. Did you not?"

"I did bring him through here," Cid says, "hoping to save him."

"A task at which you *failed*. Meaning all our lives were put at risk for nothing!"

"Very true," she says. "The boy wasn't strong enough to stand, but he was capable of killing you all."

There are a few chuckles.

"You joke, but you know the dangers of

wightdust." The Accuser grins like he's won. "You know that had anyone died here, they would have risen as a wight."

The Tree Lord gives his calm Jesus smile. This is probably the trial he'd been expecting.

My heart sinks.

Cid nods. "That's my point, actually. Your law doesn't distinguish between a leper of corpsedust or wightdust, and maybe it should. That's not my place to say, Lord. However, I should let you know that while a sprinkling of corpsedust will raise a corpse, a sprinkling of wightdust will not raise a wight. For the sentience to be properly kept intact, usually that process has to take place while the victim is still alive."

The Accuser stalks up to the platform. "Every criminal wants the law to be changed when they've been found guilty of breaking it."

Cid smirks. "I'm bringing it to your attention. I'm not an expert at your laws, and I don't know the balances you keep. I do know, however, from the survival and wellbeing of the people here, that the Tree Lord is a fair leader. I expect he'll make the right decision in regards to the laws."

The Accuser points at her with a quick, jerky motion. "Which may send you to your death! You can't pretend you're unbiased."

She holds up a hand again. "Easy, Perry Mason, don't throw out your shoulder." There is some snickering at that. "I know you're the Accuser here, and that your job is to argue a point no matter what, but even you should lose sleep at night wondering about whether the laws are fair or not. To do any less would be inhuman."

The Tree Lord gives a tired sigh. I think Cid pulled it off.

"Amirani, any questions?" the Lord asks.

For once, he decides to do a cross examination.

Amirani's black cloak sweeps around him as he walks toward her. "El Cid, how many demons have you killed?"

"That's not relevant," the Accuser steams, but Cid ignores him.

"Not enough," she says.

The crowd laughs again.

"Seriously though?" Amirani asks. "How many?"

"Thousands. Maybe tens of thousands."

"Have you killed wights before?"

She purses her lips. "They're rare, so not many. But a few."

"Would you like to kill more?"

Cid grins, bloodlust plain on her face. "Yes. Yes, I'd like that very much."

Amirani smiles back at her.

The Tree Lord's shoulders are still slumped. "Bring out the father," he says in a monotone voice.

Guards flank me as I walk across the platform. Josh is not with me, though I almost wish he was. The faces in the crowd seem more curious than judgmental. I long to believe the fate of my son is already decided, that nothing I can do or say will sway my fortunes.

What a comforting illusion that would have been.

The guards stop, and I mount the steps. Boards creak as I make my way onto the stage. A gentle breeze blows across my face in the strange silence.

I feel their eyes on me. I feel the weight of their expectation. I feel their need for judgement.

Fuck them.

They have no right to judge me. I should be

judging them.

The Tree Lord smiles. He's a thin man, and gaunt, which is odd for a leader. From a distance, I'd thought he was almost supernaturally calm, but up close he's a little twitchy. His fingers tremble as he adjusts his green cloak over his chest. A golden key, looking more medieval than modern with its circular head and uneven tines, hangs around the thong necklace he wears.

The key to the kingdom, I suppose.

The silence holds as he stares at me. A sparrow flutters by.

"So you're the one we have to thank for endangering our city?" the Accuser asks.

I survey the crowd. The redhead's eyes are the ones I catch. She's still by the cage, her face unreadable.

I return my gaze to my erstwhile Jesus.

"Son," the Accuser addresses me condescendingly, "are you going to answer the question?"

I ignore him.

The Tree Lord's face is unchanging. He leans forward. "Are you the one we have to thank for endangering our city?"

"Would you let your son die?" I ask the Tree Lord.

He raises his chin. "I don't have a son."

Oh no, fucker. You don't get off that easy. I motion to the crowd. "You're a leader. In some way, all of these people are your children. Would you let them die?"

"I'd much rather one die than many," he says.

"I agree."

I can feel the tension between us. He irrationally dislikes me in the same way that I dislike him. I'm an infidel. There has to be a way to work that to my advantage. Maybe I can make him overcompensate? Can I be the kind of person he loves to hate? Or loves to forgive?

Do I want to be forgiven?

Of course I do. I hate him, but I don't want to lose my son. Aiden can't die for my pride.

The Accuser was saying something, but I don't pay him any attention. He throws up his hands.

The Tree Lord speaks, "So you don't think you endangered my people by bringing your son here?"

"Of course I don't. Cid told you that wightdust doesn't work like corpsedust does. You probably knew that already. That may mean that you might want to switch the way you ferment your bloodwater. I'm sure your people fear the dust from the corpses."

The crowd mumbles. I'd struck a nerve. The Tree Lord's forehead creases. We did want to aim more for the people than for the Tree Lord in the hearing, so maybe I shouldn't worry that I'd put him off.

"We'll speak of that later," the Tree Lord says authoritatively, losing his Christ-like demeanor in favor of a typically Christian one. "You make a terrible assumption. It is I, for Dendra, who decides the level of danger an act causes."

"Yes, my Lord." I say. "I'm asking that you make that assessment. I was hoping you believed El Cid. If not, I'm sure her or Amirani can arrange a test for you so you can verify I did not endanger your people."

"You broke the law!" His head jerks fast enough to disturb the key on his chest. "Whether it is correct or not doesn't matter. A law is a law, even if you don't agree with it."

I see some motion out of the corner of my eye. I turn back to our cage and see Neb. He's having difficulty controlling himself.

Something the Tree Lord said must have pissed him off.

"Correct, my Lord," I say. "It's not my place to make the decision on whether you can countermand the law in the name of justice. That is for Lords and Judges. As I said, I leave that in your hands."

The Accuser speaks up. "Are you above the law, my Lord?"

The crowd goes silent again. Apparently this hasn't been decided yet.

What was the Tree Lord to say? Would he rather give up control or look like a fair leader? And is someone who blindly follows legislation fair, or just cruelly disposed in a more predictable manner?

"I have the right to pardon people," he says, which is a better answer than I would have given.

"May I?" the Accuser asks.

The Tree Lord nods, patting the key at his chest. "As you will."

The Accuser takes my measure. "You love your son?"

This time I answer. "More than anything."

"No matter what happens to him?" he asks.

Oh no. You're not fooling me with this shit. "No matter what happens. Even if I have to slay Aiden to prevent him from harming others, I will still love him."

He takes a few steps to one side, like a pacing cat, and then turns back to me. "I think you'd slay this entire village to save your son."

Damn right I would, and I'd start with you. "I value life more than that."

He laughs. "I don't think you realize how transparent you are. I don't think you realize how clear it is to everyone that you're lying."

No, sir, I'm not falling for this shit either. "I don't care if you believe me, Accuser. It's the Tree Lord's opinion that matters."

"You don't know us," the Accuser continues. "You do know your son, however."

"I have a conscience. I don't know about yours, but mine prevents me from killing people who don't deserve to die."

He paces a few more steps. "Does it?"

"It does."

He looks directly at me. "So you didn't slay an entire room full of innocent men in order to kill your wife?"

How the fuck does he know? Durgan? Did Durgan tell Keith? And then Keith told the Accuser. Jesus Christ. I feel like my soul is sinking.

But I don't care.

I don't care how many people I killed. They deserved to die anyway. They wouldn't stand up and fight Hell. They might as well have been the Archdevil's men. Evil thrives when good men do nothing, right? In Hell that means they deserve to die.

I'd fucking do it again. I would. I would. I fucking would.

Don't say I wouldn't.

There's no need for me to feel guilty.

No fucking need.

Jesus. You can't cry here, Cris.

You're fucking losing it. You can't lose it now. You're going to kill your son.

But the tears are already here.

You have to do something. You have to. You can't let him win like this. You have to lie to win.

"Not the men," I choke. "My lover. She'd turned and served the Archdevil. I had to kill her to save my son."

The Accuser spits on the square's floor. "Don't lie to me. Keith's been through Maylay Beighlay. He's seen the carnage you created."

I let the tears fall and meet his eyes. Each lie which had left my lips hurt. It felt like it had left dark stains on my soul—but there would be time enough for absolution later. Right now, good needs to win, and if not good, then I need to.

"Damn right," I say. "The Archdevil had taken that city. It had gone dark. The people who were his, I slew. The wights and the soon-to-be wights. I did not kill any innocents." I turn to Keith. "If you found the bodies of any who did not deserve to die, then those were men the Archdevil killed."

"So you claim," the Accuser says.

I roll my eyes. "Were you there?" I ask.

"And it—"

"Were you there?" I repeat.

"You don't ask the questions, you answer."

"Were you there? If you weren't, how are you pretending to know what happened? Hell, Keith wasn't even there. What did you do, look at every dead body, decide some men were good and some were bad, and then pretend you knew that I killed the good ones?"

The Accuser looks back to Keith. Keith's eyes are on me.

I can't be sure of his expression, but I think he might be afraid.

"I'd say it's awfully odd that you are the only person, good or bad, to walk away from that city," the

Accuser tries.

"You fight a fucking Archdevil," I say. "See if you can keep anyone alive."

Some in the crowd are nodding. Thank God somebody's on my side.

"May I?" Amirani asks.

The Tree Lord holds out a hand. "Be my guest."

The infidel walks up to the stage. "Would you slay your son if you thought he was beyond hope?"

The question is a set up, I know, but it stings me as badly as one of the Accuser's.

No. No I would not. "Yes," I say. "Even if he had hope, I would if I thought he was going to hurt people."

Amirani walks away, apparently satisfied.

The Tree Lord smirks. "Then before we hear from the scout, let's hear from Callodax.

Amirani stops dead in his tracks, then looks over his shoulder.

The infused steps down from the stairs the Tree Lord had used.

The Tree Lord turns and smiles on seeing him. "Keith's master. The man you claim drove the wight here."

Callodax is hairless. Not like a bald man, but lacking eyebrows and, though I can't see him clearly at this distance, I remember him not having eyelashes either. His manner of dress hasn't changed.

He's got a black, velvety-looking turtleneck that shimmers in the greenish light of Dendra. His pants are also black, but loose fitting. He wears no shoes, but instead has his feet wrapped in dark cloth.

The crowd doesn't know what to think. He certainly appears alien, and his bald head and turtleneck don't make him visually charismatic. Or maybe they do in a way. He just looks demonic. How could they mistake him for anything other than a devil?

His walk is . . . not awkward, but unique. Maybe he lifts his knees a little too high, or a little too quickly, but there's something inhuman in his measured strides.

The way he ascends the stairs to the stage is familiar. I can't quite put my finger on it, but it's as if he has too much control over his motion. He pauses, for a brief second, near the top stair of the platform—one foot still in the air—but his frame seems as well balanced as when he had both feet firmly planted.

Then he mounts the stage.

He turns to face the Tree Lord. His arrogance is not like the infidels'. It's something more sinister, more demonic—or at least it seems that way to me.

The Tree Lord gives the man a knowing smile.

"Callodax," the Tree Lord addresses the infused. "First, let me thank you for the peace. As I understand it, you attacked Varadoolyn's devils, stopping their attack on the city."

Well, that does explain why the Tree Lord thinks things are safe enough to have a hearing.

Callodax steps forward with one foot and says, "With Carrion born I've come, soldiers whose mettle has been tempered in the black depths of that most obscene labyrinth. We made short work of the devils which besieged and beleaguered your foliaged town in no small part, I assure you, because we came upon them from behind."

His speech is all wrong, and his accent is

unrecognizable. He uses a mode of speaking which doesn't seem to quite fit English grammar. Or it does, but in an odd way—as if he's trying to meet the dictates of two languages at the same time. One, ours, and the other, some demonic tongue.

The Tree Lord smiles. "Did you drive these men into our city?"

Callodax shrugs. "We gave chase for many miles, Lord of Trees and Branches, though the demons became so thick that we held back, deciding to give up pursuit in favor of attacking them on the by and by."

My heart skips a beat, and Aiden looks up.

On the by and by. I'd heard that before. And that accent . . . only I hardly recognized it because the Archdevil who spoke in that manner had seemed to be half talking in sound, and half talking to my mind.

The infused speaks like Xyn.

What had infused it? Was it really a Revenant, a soul they'd dragged back across the Erebus from Sheol? How much devil had they managed to put into the body of the man? Xyn had been a horror, not just because of his power, but because he'd found men and women who were moronic enough to follow him. But this thing, it seems human. Any old fool would follow it.

"We found these infidels holed up near the Northern wastes," Callodax is saying, "along the desolation that follows the flow of the river Erebus. We knew they harbored a wight in their stronghold, so we felt bound by virtue to strike. What flummoxes us, Lord of Trees and Branches, is that you have given them shelter. I have been tasked by Igraine herself to use her Carrion born in an attempt to slay this wretched being."

The Tree Lord gives Amirani a snide glance. "The infidels claim to have been driven here by evil men, but you and your army are not evil. It may well be that the wight will walk the plank."

Callodax shakes his head. "That will not do."

The Tree Lord's eyes widen. Is he surprised? I'm not.

Of course the fall won't satisfy the infused. Callodax doesn't want Aiden dead, he wants my boy at his side.

"To my care, deliver the wights, Durgan and Aiden," Callodax says. "If you do this, Igraine and I shall honor the deal for ammunition as discussed. Fail, as you are wont, and I and my men will no longer hold back Varadoolyn's devils." The crowd erupts, but the infused speaks right over them. "Your village for too long harbored these wights, and have done yourselves the . . . dishonor . . . of putting one on trial. You've no right to end the life of them, and have no understanding of what steps must be taken to ensure the permanence of the creatures' death."

Callodax threatened them. I can't believe he just threatened them. What a stupid fucking move. The Tree

Lord was about to happily deliver us into their hands. Why would he . . . but I don't want to underestimate Callodax. Maybe it's not some kind of demonic pride which drives him. Maybe this is just his first play. He convinced Igraine to give him some troops. He'll probably want Dendra to be under his thumb too. His dominance over Dendra could be as important to him as getting my boy.

The Tree Lord takes to his feet, a sneer on his face. "You threaten me, in my own tree?"

Callodax nods in response. "I do."

"Get out of here."

Callodax regards the masses of treemen with contempt. "You have three days to deliver the wights to me. Fail this, and you will die."

The redhead takes a breath.

I look to Cid. She's frowning.

It's the ammo. Dendra is almost out, and no doubt the infused is offering it to them at bargain basement prices. That's got to be why he thinks he has the leverage to threaten them.

"Are we okay?" I whisper.

Not looking at me, Cid says, "Cris, I think we're fucked."

XIII

The sounds of shuffling undead come down through my cell's ceiling, keeping me awake—keeping me at the mercy of my own terrible thoughts.

The sword doesn't even bother waiting for my dreams to appear anymore. It hovers above me in my cell, spinning with the tangibility of a full on hallucination, dangling precariously on that single thread.

All that has happened to me since I've come to this city, our imprisonment, the attempted rape of Cid, the trial—all of it has done nothing to stave off our doom. All it's done is put names onto the analogy of my story.

The sword is Callodax.

The horse hair is the thread of my son's goodness.

Damocles is my son—or me. Let's say it's me.

And then it strikes me that things aren't so bad. The epiphany is familiar, like that terrible moment when I realized I deserved to be in this prison.

Aiden is a wight. I knew Hell was going to take him away from me completely. I knew that the tiny piece of good in him was delicate, as delicate as a single strand of horsehair, and that the dark perversion which grips his soul would eventually take over. I knew it.

I know it.

And this development with Callodax, this is a *good* thing. When this whole journey started, I'd kept my son on edge for weeks, torturing him physically. Am I not doing a similar thing by keeping him on a moral edge now? A wight needs devils, or an infused. My son needs to be in their care. What could I or the infidels have to offer him?

I have to tell him. I have to tell him it's okay.

More than that, he's still got his faith blinders on. I need to remove them. I need to let him know how he's been manipulated.

I roll over to the wall closest to him.

I rap on it gently a few times.

"Aiden?" I whisper.

No answer.

"Aiden?" I try again.

"Quiet, Cris." His voice is raspy.

I put my hand up against the wood. "I need to tell you something. When you and Durgan were talking. When you said—"

"I hate you, Cris," he says calmly.

His words do all that a blow would. I lose my breath. I see stars. Tears form in my eyes.

He's hurting, I understand that. The trial. Seeing the infused. Durgan calling into question his entire existence.

I sit up. "You need to listen. You're about to be taken by Callodax and I—"

"I hate you."

The hell is he saying? "You need to listen, son."

"You're nothing to me. You're not my father. You're an infidel. I hate you."

How could he say this? How the hell could he say this? I've done everything for him. *Everything.*

I leap to my feet. "You've no right!" I shout. "Not after what I've done for you. Not after that. I risked my life, I risked the infidels' lives, I murdered a whole damn room of innocents just to keep you alive. I dragged a fucking Nazi across hell for you. And you *hate* me? You fucking . . . ingrate!"

His voice is calm. "You've done nothing to help me. You tried to make me human. You killed my mother. You killed my father. The only thing you ever did for me was help me finish becoming a wight. That was harder than you knew . . . but you only did it because you wanted me to become your son. I'll *never* be your son."

I'd known this was coming. I'd known Hell would get him, and it's finally taken him away from me.

I spent three years tracking Myla. I slew an Archdevil. I found a way to cure my son. I dragged him across Hell. I traversed Soulfall. In the end, I'm no better off than if I had just stayed home.

Q had known. He told me to forget my son and make another one.

That's what I should have done.

I hang my head and cry.

Nightmares of murdered innocents wake me from my slumber. It feels like I have not slept long, but who knows. The mists are thick outside, my chamber is dim, my breathing quick and shallow.

I'm covered in sweat.

I see the redhead entering, her food basket in her hands.

One of the guards nods as she enters. "Ghela," he greets her.

Was it Ghela's footsteps which woke me, and not my guilt-laden dreams?

She kneels softly beside my bars, casting a quick look over her shoulder toward the guards, red curls whipping about. Her blue eyes seem black in the dark, and her pale, slender hand reaches out to me.

We meet, palm to palm, and I feel her warmth radiating through her fingers.

"Are you okay?" she asks.

"Yes," I say.

Who knows why I said that. The only "okay" thing I can point to now is that I'm not dead yet . . . and even that's debatable considering I'm in Hell.

She passes me a bowl of devilwheat. I taste it out of politeness.

It's got some sinfruit in it.

She leans forward. "I sweetened it for you."

"Stay back from the cage, Ghela!" a treeman shouts.

"I love you," she whispers.

She's so sincere, and I feel a surge of hope at her words. She turns away, and in that last second before her face is hidden from me fully, I see her top lip twitch into a sneer.

I try to square that expression with her profession of love. Was she thinking of someone else? Was she sneering at the guard? Was she remembering her past?

I watch her walk across the prison chamber to feed Cid.

Durgan sits in his cage, unmoving, paying no attention to her.

No.

Oh fuck no.

Not again. I can't take this.

Durgan has watched everyone as they entered and exited. He paid utmost attention to every visitor. Except her. And she'd been feeding him, I remember her telling me how gross the wight's food was.

Why would he bother watching her? She's Durgan's messenger. She's one of Keith's.

And now it all made sense. It was Ghela who had snitched about my lie to Keith . . . a lie which she could not have heard because I fucking remembered her being on the vines when I passed through Dendra. Come to think of it, she's probably the reason why Amirani's witness is dead.

And of course this would happen.

Of course.

After the things I've done, don't I deserve this?

If I deserve this prison, don't I deserve my son's hate?

Don't I?

I feel like I'm going to cry again, but I don't. I'm not going to be a bitch. I don't need to cry.

I awaken, my heart thundering in my chest. There had been demons all around me. In my dream. It was just a dream.

"Cris?" Q's voice comes to me through the wall. "Cris, the hell is going on?"

These nightmares are tearing me apart.

"I'm okay," I lie again.

I look up, the treemen are by my cage. Josh looks horrified. He's stunned. Shaken. His friend pulls him away from the bars.

"Cris," Q says. "You were screaming. I thought you were dying."

I think about this. "I am. We are. We all are."

"Is it the trial?" Q says. "What's gotten you?"

What's gotten me? Really? What the fuck's gotten me? My son is lost. You fucking idiot. I've lost my only son.

My only son.

I wait for a moment, the sweat cooling on my body. Josh and the other guard move away.

"He's gone, Q." I can hear the tears in my voice.

Who would have guessed I'd spend the end of my life crying five times a day.

"Your son?" Q's voice asks me.

"Yes."

"He's been gone a long time, Cris."

I breathe in the humid air. He's right. My son has been dead a long time. But to me, he died today. "He said he hated me."

Q grunts. "Cris, I don't think you've thought this through."

"Look. Maybe I lost him a long time ago, but—"

"No, Cris. I don't think you know what it means to hear a wight say they hate you."

I think about this. About how backward wights are.

"Okay, I'm listening."

"Your son's soul is untouched. The body that looks and acts like your son, it's the result of his soul being filtered through a taint. It poisons his actions, thoughts, words and deeds. It makes evil feel like good, and good feel like evil. It makes love feel like hate.

"You've been looking at this the wrong way. When your son loved you, despite being a wight, this should have torn you apart—because now, when your son tells you he hates you, he means something else. Somewhere, wherever your son's soul is . . . he . . ."

He loves me.

The cord is thin, and it cuts into my palms . . .

But it must break. It broke before. I'd clung to it, and climbed it, hand over hand while it made mincemeat of my palms.

And it would break again.

A sword dangles from the end of it, far below me. Not the Sword of Damocles, but the sword of an infidel. It glows a soft purple.

But it must break.

It has to break.

It has to break because I'm going to use it to kill the people who want to hurt my son.

And then I'm going to kill my son, because he

wants to hurt himself too.

Men are coming down the stairs.

Am I peaceful?

No.

Come what may.

The treemen fan out into our chamber. Fabian is among them, trying to look strong and big, which probably means he's in some deep shit.

But I'm not worried about that.

Because I'm peaceful?

No. I'm not. Because I'm warlike.

Come what may.

The bells jingle. Iron squeaks against green wood as the three bars of my prison rise. As always, they only come up a few feet.

I stretch, and notice I am protected from my agony by something. The pain in me is a distant thing, shouting alone, lost in some cave, destined to die as Hell irrevocably heals my wounds.

The infidels taught me a few sit out drills during our wrestling classes. I walk to the bars and use the maneuver to slip through the tiny opening. I come to my feet, bouncing. I'd been wrong about my body—it feels good. Damn everything else. I feel good.

My body moves, almost as if propelled by the will

of some god of vengeance, walking with the others up the stairs. The world around it passes in a blur as we retrace our steps.

Josh is saying something to me.

I look to him.

"I said, for what it's worth, I respect you."

I nod.

Psychopomps soar through the open, slightly humid air. The breeze whispers around us with the gentle murmur of leaves, branches and birds. The mists below diffuse the abyss' illumination enough to give us an even lighting. Cid seems well. Her swelling is completely gone, and the scabs on her face give a good contrast to her preternaturally pale skin.

Neb is slow, as stiff as a board.

But not me.

Something has changed. Something deep within me has begun to understand.

We travel down to the Prima Tree. My sight is on point. I notice some of the tiniest details which I missed before . . . like the infidel marked panel behind the gate where the Tree Lord will enter. It reminds me of the panel Cid had used to drop the armory in our safe chamber.

That's where Amirani must have installed the trigger to jettison the tree.

Wouldn't that be something.

The crowd has beat us here. They stand across the

platform. I recognize some of the faces. The strained, pained face of Fabian's wife. The gorgeous red curls of Ghela. The narrow face of the Accuser.

I see the huge hanging counterweights they use to bring barrels up into the Prima Tree, each nearly touching, this one slightly lower than that one on the ends of their pulleys.

They take us to the cage . . . all of us, save Aiden.

And there, entering with Keith on one side and a darkly dressed Carrion born soldier on his left, is Callodax, the infused. My son's future father.

I take in a deep breath. Am I at peace with this?

He can raise my son to be the wight he was meant to be . . . but there is something else in the back of my mind. My intuition is going mad. Everything I've ever learned about Hell is that no matter how well I perform, no matter how many demons I kill, no matter what lands I traverse, I will always somehow lose. But I can't believe it. My heart beats. I feel like I can win. Like Hell will break.

It's best not to lie to oneself.

But I can't shake the feeling.

Hope springs eternal . . . but in the endless pit of Hell, an eternal spring is just a drop of spittle in a gaping canyon.

Yes.

But the feeling won't go away.

Aiden is not taken to the cage like we are. He is

brought to the platform.

He seems calm. His hate has made him strong. He has nothing to fear with Callodax. Nothing at all. Maybe he's figured that out already.

The Tree Lord had not slept well. I see the lines of worry on his Jesus face. So, Son of God, did you decide to make a deal with the Devil, or not? Are you smart enough to sense your own destruction?

Aiden marches up the stairs and stands defiant, hands behind his back, his feet apart . . . much like an infidel might. Ghela stands next to me, just beside my bars.

The Tree Lord rises. "You've all heard the threat, made here yesterday. I have spoken more with Callodax, and come to understand the source of his ire. Please remember also that his was a threat of inaction. He merely means to say that if we do not trust him, that he will not be our ally."

There is some mumbling.

A quick glance at Callodax's face reveals nothing.

The Tree Lord glances toward us. No. Not toward us. Toward Ghela. Wait, she's not his agent—but I get the feeling from the Tree Lord's glance that he *thinks* she is. I'm amazed by how much I underestimated her. Maybe it's because Igraine was right and I'm a sexist bastard. Maybe it's because I can't imagine someone who is not an infidel being this powerful. But I cannot be a fool any longer. This woman is my enemy.

"I have agreed, then," the Tree Lord says, "to include the young wight as payment in our ammunition deal with Callodax and his mistress, Igraine. He will be delivered on the morrow, along with our barrels of sap and bloodwater upon receipt of the ammunition."

Amirani stiffens. "You have not pronounced judgement on the wight. I assume that if you want to change his execution from the fall to extradition, you would first have to find him guilty."

The Tree Lord sits down. "I pronounce him guilty."

"We've not finished the trial," Amirani points out.

"He's had enough of one," the Tree Lord says.

"It barely started!"

I cloak myself in calm. You could have had it differently, Tree Lord. I'm sorry for what I'm going to do to you.

The Tree Lord bangs one fist against his throne's arm. "He's a wight. He needs no trial. Only people need trials."

"He's attached to a human soul."

"Enough!" the Tree Lord pounds his fist again. "I summarily find all dyitzu guilty as well, but you and I can argue the finer points of that later." He comes back to his feet. "As for the infidels, I understand that their behavior is not just reprehensible for a person of Dendra, but for their own kind as well. For this reason I have decided to send for *the* Infidel . . . or someone high enough in their standing to carry weight. Ares,

Endymion, Huginn or Muninn. Someone of that nature. They will advise me of what kind of judgement *they* think you should have."

Ah, that's their game. Callodax is trying to lure high powered infidels here, probably to kill them.

I look to Ghela. Her sneer is back, a victorious one this time. The Tree Lord has been played.

Oh, sure, it looks like he's made the right decision. In his mind, all Callodax has over him are the devils his men are "keeping at bay." The Tree Lord knows that a crew of infidels would happily wipe out the devils at the edge of his village. Ares would be a particular treat. The Order are scared shitless of him, and I can't imagine the Carrion born have a different opinion.

Callodax inclines his head and takes a few steps forward, wry amusement in his smile.

Whichever infidel comes is walking into an ambush.

I look up and see the sword.

Break, little string.

Come what may.

I turn to Ghela, grasping the hilt of Damocles' sword. "Make sure you feed me tonight. I have news," I whisper.

She nods in agreement.

The string breaks. The sword is mine.

Callodax, you are my weapon.

In the dark of night I hear her soft steps on the wooden stairs. Come to me. You've helped write Callodax's play so far. It's time to write a few lines for me.

Ghela passes between the guards, walks by Aiden's cage and comes to me. As always, Durgan appears to ignore her.

Her cruel face is covered in shadow. She kneels by the bars, her burlap clothes settling around her. She offers me the food.

"Leave the city tonight," I tell her. "Wait for us by the Northern Lethe. We'll be there in the pre-dawn, right when the silver light returns."

She frowns. "Oh, Cris. The Tree Lord won't let you escape."

I smile. "No. We're not escaping, we're being let go! The Tree Lord is playing Callodax for a fool. Ares came in last night and struck a deal with the Tree Lord. Amirani has no need to go get Ares—you understand? Ares is already here. We're being freed, the boy included, tomorrow just before first light. The Tree Lord didn't like Callodax's threat, and our freedom was the price he paid for infidel protection."

Shock, naked and real, hits her, widening her pupil-filled eyes.

I keep my face earnest. "You've been kind to me. I know you must hate Dendra. Come away with me."

Slowly, her mouth slightly ajar, she holds up the

water.

I drink it. She lets me have way too much.

"Will you meet me here or at the river?" I ask. "I don't actually know where on the river Ares will be, so it would be better here."

She doesn't answer. She doesn't go to feed the others. She sprints out of the room.

I stretch my muscles.

Come what may.

"Where's my food!" I shout.

The guards, confused by Ghela's sudden departure, step to where they can see me.

"Where is it?" I yell.

I rush them, slamming my body against the bars. The bells jingle in protest.

Josh isn't on duty now, for which I'm thankful. He kind of likes me. I'd hate to disabuse him of his affection.

I step back to give myself some space and charge the bars once more.

Again the bells greet me.

I scream, letting my real anger escape.

"Stop!" the first guard yells.

"He's cracked," the other says.

I see Cid looking up at me from where she lays in her cell. Neb is confused, perhaps unsure of whether I'm acting, or if I really have lost it.

Oh, have a little faith, my Nazi friend.

"Stay back!" the first guard warns, raising his rifle to his shoulder.

I turn and rush the outward facing bars, slamming into them, screaming madly.

It's not a hard act. My rage is uncontainable. It flows through me like a river. I hit the bars again.

"You'll kill yourself!" a guard screams. "Stop."

I hear the sound of the corpses above me. I jump, reaching upward through the bars, shouting, until one of them catches my arm.

I grip it back.

I use the limb to pull my entire body up. I place my feet upon the ceiling and then jump downward.

The arm crackles and I hear the snapping of undead tendons. The arm holds. I put my feet back up and jump again. With a snap and the sound of shorn paper, the arm rips free. The wood floor is as hard as concrete, but the pain of the impact doesn't bother me. I toss the corpse arm aside and charge the outside bars again.

I rebound off them and collapse by the wall where Fabian's bullet had impacted.

The tears in my eyes are both fake and real.

The guards watch me cry for maybe five minutes before they return to their posts.

From slamming into the cage, I have a good idea which bars are the weakest. I rip off the skin from the undead arm and crush it, letting the corpse dust fall at the base of the two bars I've decided on.

I remove a shard of Fabian's bullet from the wall, but my grip isn't strong enough to chip away at the wood with it. I bite on my thumbnail to clip it just a little, jam the shard under my nail, and press it down into the wood to set it in my flesh.

The pain shouts to me, a wailing woman in a far off land.

I hunch over, pretending to cry as cover while I work at the base of the bars, using the broken piece of the bullet to dig up splinters. This lets the corpsedust settle more deeply around the bars.

"Cris." Q's voice calls to me.

I imagine his face.

I've shared nothing of my plan with him. How much of what I'm doing does he understand?

In my mind's eye, his face is warm, caring. He has faith in me.

I hear the distant quiet tinkle of a disturbed bell, and then silence. Q must be grabbing one of the bars nearest my cage.

"Remember Maylay Beighlay?" he asks me.

Of course I do.

"Cris, hell could hardly hold you then," Q says. "You had only a little knowledge, and barely any training. Imagine what will happen when you face it now."

He knows. He doesn't think I've lost my mind.

And his words are exactly what I want—no, what I *need* to hear. Those are the words that give life and logic to my intuition—to the idea that I can finally win.

I redouble my fake tears and work as the blood of my thumbnail mixes in with the corpsedust and sawdust.

I hear Aiden's sneering voice from across the wall. "You're a weakling father."

Q knows me better than my own son.

I whisper back to him. "Somewhere beyond your body, you can hear me. I'm coming for you again, Aiden. Do you understand? I'm coming, and there is nothing in this Hell, not on Earth or in Heaven—not man, not woman, not devil—that can stop me."

My work done, I lay down in the darkness.

I close my eyes and rest.

The rest isn't really sleep because my day has only just begun. Rather, I feel almost meditative. It reminds me of a long commute in an old world morning, when the traffic is light and the sky is dark. My body feels good. My muscles loose. My wounds healed.

I know what you want, Callodax. You want my son. How much do you want him?

You're out there, I know it.

Ghela has surely found you by now. You're in a hurry, getting your forces ready. There isn't much time, she's told you. Aiden escapes in the morning, she's told you. The boy will be out of your reach and the infidels will be free.

I can't know your motivation, Callodax. I know only that you came from Soulfall, and that you might have come from Sheol before that. I know you've tried to kill us without fail ever since then. But will you come now?

Somehow I know you will. Whatever hints about your character I've picked up in our brief interactions, I can say at least this, you want Aiden.

But I want him more. More than anyone. More than anyone has ever wanted anything.

I breathe in and out. When I breathe in, I imagine a brilliant light of purifying power, and when I breathe out, I imagine exhaling a black cloud of my own weakness.

Come what may, I'll kill it.

I feel the change in the light before my eyes can detect
it.

The routine sound of boots on the stairs, a guard
change and nothing more, adds an air of militarism to
the queer silence which hangs over us like a blanket,
muffling the whispering leaves and the oh-so-gentle
breeze. I rise. Was I ever sore? Had I ever been
wounded? Has anything ever hurt me?

I cannot know.

The guards exchange a soft perfunctory greeting as
their shift changes. One of the new men is Josh. Maybe I
know this because I've memorized the schedule. Maybe
I know this because I can detect the fact that he favors

one foot on the stairs. Maybe the Devil told me.

Lightly, as if I were an infidel, I come to the inner bars.

Blood drips from where I had previously embedded the bullet shard in my thumbnail, splattering against the wooden floor beneath me.

Josh is disheveled. Tired. Torn.

It will not get better for him.

He looks at me.

"You can feel it, can't you?" I ask him.

His friend freezes. Even insane infidels like myself are dangerous. Even caged ones. Even ones doomed to die.

"Don't listen to him," the treeman advises Josh. "He's fucking with you. He's trying to get under your skin."

Josh's eyes are glued on me.

I cock my head to one side and listen. "It's in the breeze, don't you think? Or maybe you can feel its vibrations, coming through the stones and into the trees. It's in the way the birds have stayed silent this morning."

Josh stops, also cocking his head to listen. His friend starts to speak, but then pauses, perhaps entertaining my suggestion.

"It's coming," I tell him. "That thing you fear. The attack. The devils. Callodax's army of thugs, fools and demons. They're coming."

Josh's friend grabs his arm, trying to turn him away.

Josh shakes himself loose, his eyes focused on me.

"When it comes," I tell him. "You'll need to let me go."

"See!" his friend shouts. "He's trying to get in your head."

The shout dies, sucked away by the quiet. There is the breeze. A single, hesitant chirp . . . and then silence.

Josh swallows hard enough that I can see his Adam's apple bobbing in the near darkness.

"You'll need to let me go," I continue, "because without me, your people will lose. You won't survive this, Josh. Nor will your family."

His friend grabs his arm again. "Don't listen!"

I step close to the bars, so close I can feel the cool air surrounding the iron on my cheek.

"If you do not listen," I tell him, "then run. Gather those you love and get out while you still can."

Josh turns away. His shoulders are rising with his heavy breathing. That man is terrified. Good. He should be. My hell is coming.

And for a perfect minute, all around us is that eerie tension before a battle.

The wind whispers to me. "You are mortal," it says. "Never forget you are mortal."

Fuck you, wind.

Then, even as the first signs of light begin to breach

the lower mists, the explosion rips across the chamber. It's not like the small points of demolition caused by our infidel fire—no. Not at all.

The boom is a horrific thunderous crack which sounds out like a mountain splitting, echoing in a horrid, repetitive staccato across the chamber as it's shockwave shakes the trees. The birds cry out as rock shrapnel pummels the trunks and rips through the leaves. Dust fills the chamber as the gentle rain of silt descends through the air, some of it billowing through the outer bars and into my room.

I do not move as it swirls around me.

Josh and the treeman have dropped, taking cover in their fear. Josh's eyes are wide. He stares up at me.

"Callodax is here," I say.

His friend stands, tugging at him, shouting— though the voice seems small after such an apocalyptic clamor—pleading. "Your family, Josh! My daughter! We've got to get them out. Leave this infidel. Leave Fabian. Let's leave this whole damn place."

Josh shakes his head. "We have to fight." He turns to me. "I'm sorry."

I shrug.

Josh and his friend rush away, but it is no matter.

I learned how to throw a sidekick back on Earth, but I never really used it much. El Cid had tweaked the way I threw it. The power, she taught me, is in the moment when I shift my weight on the ball of my planted foot. The kick is strongest when that shift comes just slightly earlier than I'd been executing.

I sidekick the ever-living shit out of a bar I'd weakened with my careful chipping and application of corpsedust. With the dull ring of iron and the sudden crack of rotten wood, the first bar falls free. It rings as it hits the wood, rolling and tumbling down until it settles on the wide smooth branch below.

With similar force, I kick out the second bar.

The treemen are shouting, though I can't see them through the thick mists. Already I hear the distant hiss of dyitzu and the sizzle of their incoming fireballs.

I look behind me.

Cid, Neb, and Durgan are all staring at me.

I meet Durgan's glassy, black eyes. "All ye all ye out and free."

Cid is smiling.

I remember something she told me once.

I have to turn your blood into lava and your body into whetstone. I have to turn your mind into a raging current of lightning, your will into an avalanche, your soul into a wellspring. And then, when you have learned to despise Hell, when you know her weaknesses, when you know how to break her, then I have to unleash you.

I leap through the breach.

XVIII

The grey bark slopes out beneath me as I slide along. Broken pieces of it shower down around me. Where the trunk meets the branch-formed landing, I roll and come to my feet.

The particulate of the explosion and the heavy morning mist hang together in the air, forming a shifting haze which swallows the edges of my vision. From where I stand, I can just barely see the hanging vines of sinfruit against the grey wall of forever. Despite my limited visibility, I know the fight is on. I hear the howls of hounds and the hiss of dyitzu. I hear the flap of leathery wings in the air and the rush of the last remaining showers of dirt as they make their way down through the canopy. I hear the sorrow of dying men and women.

The haze mutes Dendra's illumination so evenly it seems to come from nowhere. All is colorless here except for the small red bubbles of light that paint the distant mists with streaks of sunset pink.

That's dyitzu fire.

At my feet lies one fallen bar from my cell. I put one of Jessica's boots under it and kick it up into my hand. I make my way to the vines. Then, from behind, I hear with perfect clarity the increasingly loud flapping of approaching winged devils.

I duck into the hanging sinfruit and look out, hoping the flora will give me enough cover.

Three dezendyitzu break through the walls of grey, flying in a triangular formation. Two alight on the landing where I just stood. The third hovers mightily in the air above them, its huge wings swirling the mists as it struggles to keep its dyitzu-shaped body in the air. A fourth creature, an Icanitzu, coalesces out of the mist. Its flight is more graceful, and when it hovers, it does so with less effort. The three dezens each loose a trio of fireballs. These aren't the typical dyitzu red. Dark blue and purple baubles of fire erupt from their hands, spinning unpredictably across the expanse, tearing into the vines and sending them swaying this way and that. Their multicolored flames drip down through the vines, curling the leaves into black stumps, boiling the juices out of the sinfruit and filling the air with the smell of burning sugar.

A purple tongue of fire rolls down, inches from my face. Its heat is spectacularly intense upon my cheek and eye, but I'm as still as God's conscience.

The Icanitzu barks a short command. The two dezendyitzu who landed fight their way back into the air and the wicked foursome continue on through the mists.

I hear men's shouts and the reports of gunfire. I hear the twangs of bows. I hear the whine of a wounded hound.

To climb, I tuck my iron bar under my left arm, wrapping my legs around one vine and pushing up with my feet to compensate for the limited use of my left hand. As I reach the supporting branches of the sinfruit vines, I see a dull red glow, larger than the globes of dyitzu fire, through the haze.

One of the trees is burning.

Ash, either from that, or from the vines, is drifting on the breeze. I can't see far, but I think the supporting branch curves around to the front of the prison tree. Then there should be a bridge that will take me to my equipment. But I only know this from memory. To look at it, this grey branch leads off into the never.

I can just now begin to make out tiny grey shapes ahead. I hold my iron bar before me like a tightrope walker and move quickly across the dewy branch.

Those shapes become visible as a cluster of dyitzu, maybe five of them, spread out across a wide limb, hurling their fire at a wicker bunker in the tree. One unfortunate archer lays between the two groups, smoldering. As I approach, distant fireballs, again visible only as ruddy bubbles of light, streak through the fog—but this time they're headed straight down. There must be devils crawling on the ceiling as well.

One of the five dyitzu turns to me as I near it, a fireball already formed. It throws.

Oh, you poor devil, you have no idea.

Fifty feet.

I slip the fireball, lowering my right shoulder and slowing my approach. One of his friends also focuses on me. If I can distract enough of them, the men in the bunker will get free shots at their backside. The pair looking at me tosses their fire. The dyitzu fireballs come as if in slow motion. One misses naturally, and I do a quick wide step, bending at the waist to avoid the other.

Twenty feet.

The first devil tries again as I near the pair. The branch is wide enough here to allow me some lateral movement. I spin to one side, swinging the bar at the passing fireball, hitting it from behind. The missile bursts, sending a burning napalm-like substance showering out in a wide arc behind me. Some of the flaming goo sticks to the end of my bar. I continue the spin, picking up more power before leveling a blow at a devil. The dyitzu does its best to block, but the burning iron bats its arms aside. I hear the iron ring with an almost bell-like sound as my makeshift staff impacts with its skull. Brained, the devil falls into the depths.

The four remaining dyitzu have all turned to me. I weave my way through their fireballs, staying away from their reaching claws. I see the archers in the wicker bunker stand, suddenly free of the barrage of fire. Arrows find the backs of two dyitzu. I dart at one of the surviving devils.

I hit it forcefully in the side with the butt of my staff. It bends over when I strike it, clutching the iron bar, heedless of the fire. I let it have the bar and front kick it off the branch.

Instinctively, I duck, but there was no need. The remaining dyitzu had been felled by the treemen. They look at me uneasily from their bunker.

I hold up a hand and wink at them.

I pick up the discarded bow of their smoldering comrade. The quiver is mostly in good shape, though some of the arrows' fletching had blackened from the heat. I strap the quiver around my waist. I put three arrows in my bow hand and keep a fourth ready.

Unlike the infidel-made arrows, these have very narrow notches. I go ahead and nock my free one, because it will be hard to fire these quickly.

I have to make a decision. Do I rescue my friends first, or go for my weapons? Josh and the other guard have left, but there are other treeman in the Wicker Tree who might want to put me back in my cage.

In the mist, I find myself disoriented, but after a moment to get my bearings, I'm sure I know the path to the Storage Tree.

It's eerily peaceful here, walking across the vine bridge to the Storage Tree. Reports of gunfire echo in from the direction of the Prima Tree. Men I cannot see shout, coordinating battle maneuvers over the cries of Icanitzu. Fire crackles in the distance, and the air is thick with the smell of burning plant matter. But for all that, this vine-bridge I walk along is abandoned. It's as narrow as any of the bridges in Dendra, and I have to put one foot in front of the other as if I'm walking along a balance beam. The support rails do little to make me feel any safer.

The first of the Storage Tree's dark shadowy branches emerges from the grey, and for a brief moment, I get a sense of vertigo. With only the outermost branch visible to my eyes, the tree looks like it's from the old world. Because of the distance, I can't tell its size, and since the mist obscures its trunk, I can't tell that it grows downward.

For some reason I feel terror, sheer and naked, building up inside of me. It's been collecting in my soul for all these days of anxious imprisonment—collecting for all these years I've been in Hell. I've been wounded deeply, my lovely, lovely Myla. I've lashed out at my friends. I've killed men I shouldn't have. I let this place turn us against each other.

How many others, facing up against the sublime power of some merciless enemy, have felt this terror in their gut?

She loves me. She loves me. I am not alone.

And like some gothic gargoyle springing forth from Notre Dame, an Icanitzu soars through the fog-laden branches, two dezendyitzu in tow. Men are shouting, fireballs sear through the air and arrows answer back through the haze.

On Earth, a soldier like me could steel his soul with the idea of heaven. With the knowledge that God would make sure the good guy wins. With the raw power of faith. But what of me? I've turned my back on God. I have no faith. I'm probably not even the good guy.

I'm only . . .

. . .

a man.

The silence is overtaken by the howls of devils. The tree ahead shakes in the gentle breeze of the cavern and with the travails of combat. To my left I see darkly clad soldiers, shotguns in hand, moving along another bridge.

Callodax's men have come to call.

Do they see me? Do they care? Do I?

The trunk emerges from the ashen air as I

approach, and I see that quite a few of the treemen are in its branches. The battle is being fought in earnest on the far side, but I can worry about that later. I can see the Wicker Tree back across the gap as I step upon one of the Storage Tree's landings. The haze must be clearing because I couldn't see across when I was on the other side.

There, one green-cloaked man and a cadre of white-cloaked soldiers enter, perhaps heading down to our cells.

Damn.

There's no way I can get back in time. I just have to trust that Cid can save Aiden, or hope that Fabian's not there to kill my son. It would seem wasteful to kill someone that the attacking force wants. Maybe they'll think to barter him.

A pack of dyitzu comes around the trunk and walks full force into a flurry of arrows from a nest of treemen. Two of the devils fall, and the rest head back for cover. An Icanitzu swoops down on a different nest of defenders and comes up with a man in its talons. The devil drops him into the abyss. Arrows follow, but the dezendyitzu cover the Icanitzu with their wings, and the arrows bounce off. They can only defend like that for a second though, because when they use their wings as shields they can't keep altitude.

The three swoop down, a slave to their momentum, and plummet away from the nest.

Away from the nest, and toward . . . me.

I fire an arrow directly at one of the winged dyitzu, and just as I'd seen before, it shields itself with its wings. The damn narrow notch on my next arrow nearly misses the string, but I get it loaded in time. As soon as the dezendyitzu spreads its wings to fly, I hit it straight in the face.

It plummets, clawing at the shaft buried into its cheek.

The Icanitzu screeches, its backward jointed talons reaching toward me. The remaining dezendyitzu flies upward, and I see its twisting balls of blue fire cutting through the air. My third arrow isn't ready in time. I duck the fireballs and throw the bow at the Icanitzu.

The pair swoop by, the Icanitzu crushing my bow in its talons. Weaponless, I realize just how helpless I am on this bridge.

The two devils make an immediate turn behind me as I rush ahead.

Why the hell did I throw the bow?

They glide forward, and again the dezendyitzu pulls up and looses fire. The balls curve in their flight through the air, twisting as they pass the diving Icanitzu. I turn around so I'm moving backward along the bridge, still heading to the Storage Tree. The Icanitzu flares its wings, slowing its descent as the fireballs roar by. I'm not going to be able to duck low enough to get beneath the Icanitzu.

I grab one of the rail's vertical support ropes and swing under the braided-vine bridge.

The Icanitzu claws at the empty air as I use my momentum, swinging like a monkey, to come back up from the other side.

It hovers like it's going to land, but we've moved far enough up the bridge that it's in range of the treeman nest. It darts off through the rain of incoming arrows.

The dezen tries throwing another pair of fireballs, but I avoid them easily. It hovers in the air, unwilling to leave, but unwilling to come any closer to the nest behind me.

"Don't worry," I say. "I'll be back for you."

I untie the quiver from around my waist, toss it aside, and run for the Storage Tree.

A cloud of steam and smoke, billowing forth from a dozen places where frantic treemen pour buckets of water onto their burning nests, does its best to replace the slowly thinning haze left by the initial explosion.

One man points his arrow at me. I raise my hands, but keep running forward.

"We were set free to help!" I shout.

I'm not sure how believable that lie is. If that were true, wouldn't I have some fucking weapons?

But the man seems to buy it. Even if he doesn't believe me, pretending is probably the best thing he can do right now. The last thing Dendra needs is another enemy.

The fighting is thickest near the bottom of the tree. Dyitzu seem to have overrun parts of the lower canopy, and the occasional stray fireball rises up from the fray. I see a line of their red colored bodies climbing up along the trunk. There's about a dozen of them.

Not my problem.

I spot an entrance to the Storage Tree. A dyitzu is coming out of it.

You, motherfucker, are my problem.

It sees me, and as I'm the only human not hiding in a nest on this godforsaken tree, I shouldn't be surprised that it hurls its fire at me. Infidel training has made these missiles seem slow, almost pointless. I slip it easily. The branch under my feet is thick, and the bark here provides excellent traction. I advance toward the dyitzu. It has no idea what's coming.

It tries one more fireball, but it's off target and I don't even have to dodge that one. Then it strikes at me, swinging with its claws in wide, circular attacks. I step back, letting the first two blows go by before blocking the third and countering with a short right hook. The punch lands like a blessing, rocking the devil. True to its nature, it strikes again. I duck under its claw, stepping off at one angle with my lead foot before pivoting around it in an textbook display of infidel footwork. It spins quickly, trying to get itself in line with me.

It succeeds in getting itself in line with my straight right.

Again, the blow lands solidly.

It stumbles backward, its claws slicing into the bark of the trunk, before losing its balance. It rises quickly, just in time for me to sidekick the thing off the branch.

Infidel, whoever the fuck you are, you taught your people well. This shit is amazing. I wheel about and head into the Storage Tree.

My shadow, cast before me by the dappled light of Dendra, jaggedly descends the tree's carved steps until it's swallowed by the darkness. I follow it.

The dyitzu I just fought came from down here, so I'm not surprised to hear the sounds of combat echoing up through the chambers. The stairway bottoms out into a large hollow similar to where an old world owl might have lived except much, much larger. The hollow's opening has been boarded up. Lines of grey illumination pierce through the tiny gaps of the boards and filter through the room, alighting on a series of wine barrels, dried foodstuffs and piles of the dyitzu skin smocks the Dendran people wear. No sign of my shit.

The room is large, perhaps forty feet wide, and has two exits, not counting the stairs I just descended.

Hell. Which way to go?

Firelight brightens the archway of the exit on the left. A dyitzu's missile speeds into the room. I dart to one side. It bursts on the steps, creating a small conflagration. Three dyitzu enter.

Okay, this is going to be a problem.

I charge at them, swinging. The first narrowly dodges the strike while his two friends form fireballs. Too much, I can't fight three at once.

I keep running, choosing the right exit, fire on my heels.

Shouts of human agony come from ahead. I leap over a wounded treeman, casting a look over one shoulder. There's desperation in the fallen man's eyes. I duck, and fire explodes on the wall in front of me, droplets of the burning liquid landing on my Icanitzu hide armor. It seems to be fire resistant, which is nice. The corridor takes a left turn, and so do I. Behind me the fallen man screams as the dyitzu get to him.

Sorry, my friend.

Two more of Dendra's soldiers come in from the corridors ahead. One has a pistol, the other a bow.

"My things!" I shout. "The Tree Lord sent me here. Where are my things?"

The man with a pistol has lost his wicker helmet. His bushy eyebrows furrow.

"Don't know!" says his friend, pointing behind him. "Imps down there. Run with us."

Fuckers.

I pass them by.

There's a row of doors in the next hallway. Hopefully one has my shit, but this corridor opens into another which also has some doors. Treemen flee along the other hallway, and I see a three foot golden pigmaditz pass by after them, climbing along the ceiling.

I take a look at the first door. It's got a lock. I'm fucking sure Amirani made it. I try the knob, but no luck.

Not good.

Here's to hoping Amirani didn't make the door too.

I step back and try to kick through it, aiming right beside the lock. The door bursts open. Heaps of the processed, sticky spider silk they use for their temporary bridges are packed in here, some of them creatively stuck to the ceiling. No luck at all.

The next door takes two kicks.

Processed lumber and other building materials.

Next door—a dozen pigmaditz are coming right for me, two climbing along one wall. Their black dyitzu-like eyes reflect the dim light of the hallway. Those eyes are narrow, closer set over their tiny beaks than would seem natural.

I race into the room with the building materials, slamming the door on the first pigmaditz that tries to make it through, crushing it against the door frame. I'm not sure if it's alive or just twitching, so I slam the door on it again. Another of the imps, one crawling on the wall, takes the opportunity to attack me, leaping and spreading its wings.

I step to the side and pick up a two by four. At first, I'm dismayed when the board breaks over the pigmaditz's head, but then I think better of it and jam the splintered end into its ugly, golden, beak-face. The little fuckers pour into the room. I punch, kick, bite, and scream my way out, picking one of them up by its tiny, clawed foot, using it to bludgeon the next imp in my path. They follow me out of the room cautiously. Their attempted bites and clawing hadn't done much to my Icanitzu armor, and they were understandably cautious, particularly the one with a splinter in its eye.

I toss my pigmadizt-cum-club into the room with the spider silk. The pigmaditz sticks to the back wall.

One gets brave, climbs the side of the corridor, and launches itself at me. I step off at an angle and level a Muay Thai kick into it. The crack of my shin crushing its beak resonates through the hallway. They're on me again, just like the half-rotten kids in Maylay Beighlay, two of them climbing my leg. I wrench one free and toss it into the room, kick at the group to keep them at bay, and then bludgeon the shit out of the remaining hanger-on with my fists.

Again, the armor is protecting me. I can see where their claws broke through the polished outermost shell of the leather, but none has drawn blood yet.

I hear the shouts of people behind me, and the pigmaditz break and run. Time for door number three. Wicker.

Four. Meat.

Five—last room. Dried sinfruit and brineberries.

That was the whole hallway.

I start on the door closest to me in the next corridor.

Jackpot.

My pack, so familiar and worn, sits there in one corner like the Holy Grail. My M-16 leans against it like a Lost Treasure of Atlantis. My Old Lady protrudes from its side holster like the Hand of God. My friend's packs are there too, so as I sling mine on, I raid Q's stash of infidel fire.

Another crew of imps passes down the hallway. One turns, notices me and hisses.

I pull out my Old Lady. She's a Smith & Wesson Model 916A pump action 12 gauge shotgun with a 28 inch barrel.

Are there shells in there? I can't remember, so I test it at the imp.

I blow a fist sized hole through its torso.

Yup, it's loaded, and apparently with slugs.

Here, here, little piggies, I've got something for you.

Pigmaditz blood and brains scatter to the tune of the booms of my Old Lady as I come into the hallway. When my shells have been spent, I grab the shotgun by its smoking hot barrel and Babe Ruth the next two on my way through the corridor.

I reload as I pass the spider silk room. The caught

pigmaditz stares down at me from where its stuck on the ceiling. I toss in a canister of infidel fire and close the door.

I run along the hallway to the hollow as the whistle comes to a climax.

The hollow room is thick with battle. Men hide behind barrels of bloodwater on the left while dyitzu take cover behind similar barrels on the right. The infidel fire goes off behind me.

Walking in with measured steps, I loose shotgun blasts at the dyitzu's position. More dyitzu are streaming in, coming down the stairs, fireballs forming.

I don't have time for this.

With a quick twist I open another canister of infidel fire and lob it into the midst of the bloodwater barrels. It whistles for a moment before flooding the dark room with smoke and fire, turning the chamber into a tenebristic baroque nightmare.

The alcohol of the bloodwater catches in fits, sending short-lived waves of flame flashing across the room. A dyitzu, missing one arm, comes at me through the firelight. I blast its knee with a round of buckshot, and it falls into the puddles of intermittently burning bloodwater.

I walk over its twitching body, my eyes stinging. The bloodwater sloshes under my boots and the heat makes my skin tingle. Then I'm free of the chamber. I take the stairs three at a time leaving behind me the cries of men and dyitzu.

I load the Old Lady and holster her in my pack as I top the stairs. The booms of other shotguns echo back and forth across Dendra as I step into the light. Everything is clearer now, and the haze which had previously been so thick remains only as lingering wisps. Finally, I get a feel for the scope of the battle.

The cliff wall on the west by the Prima Tree shows the blasted out hollow of a new cave. Long bridges of newly built scaffolding cross over to the branches. That must be how the Carrion born breached the chamber and crossed over into the trees. I think, even at this distance, I can see the Tree Lord in his green robe, hiding in the back of a nest. The fighting seems thick over there, as the Tree Lord's men have access to the armory and ammunition. I'm surprised he hasn't dropped the tree yet. He must not have been able to fight his way back to the safe room.

And I'm pretty sure I see Keith. Damn. That's got to be him. He's half a mile or so away, but yeah, that's him.

The trees and nests immediately surrounding the Prima Tree are occupied by devils and Carrion born. Arrows arc back and forth from tree to tree and from nest to nest as the defenders of Dendra, bolstered by their citizens, loose their quaint barrages toward the devils and Carrion born. Their enemies, better armed, but perhaps held back by their lack of familiarity with this insane environment, return fire with buckshot and fireballs. Where once psychopomps crossed the vast expanses of air between branches, pigmaditz glide this way and that, raiding nests which are otherwise unreachable to the enemy.

Dezendyitzu and Icanitzu, less daring, but far more dangerous, hover here and there behind their troops, sometimes darting in their V formations toward a nest.

To my left, in the row of trees connected to the Wicker Tree, I see the devils have made little progress. Here and there dyitzu fireballs sizzle through the air, but the wicker-helmed men and their civilian allies seem to have them mostly pinned.

I see Fabian now, his white-cloaked men flanking

him, exiting the Wicker Tree. He's got Aiden with him.

You motherfucker.

I watch his progress as I unsling my M-16.

Should I shoot them down?

What are you doing, Fabian? What do you want with my boy? Does the Tree Lord want you to try to trade him like in the original deal? Or are you guys so stubborn you're attempting to keep him safe out of spite?

I'm guessing it's the latter.

The Safe Tree, that's where they'll be taking Aiden. I'm near the center of Dendra, and the Safe Tree is about a dozen bridges away in the back corner of the complex. I see no devils climbing on the polished stone walls in that corner. The Safe Tree isn't even under attack.

If I'm quick, I bet I can beat Fabian there.

I step out onto a branch and immediately see a problem. I have enemies everywhere. I kneel, thus far unnoticed by friend or foe, taking careful aim at a nested Carrion born whose unfortunate luck it was to be along my route. He's out of range of the Dendran short bows, but he's easy pickings for my assault rifle. I switch to single shot, take aim, and loose a round.

The wicker next to him vaporizes into dust. Confused, his distant head looks back and forth. My next shot takes him in the neck. I fire again, this time at a different nest and this time with much better aim.

I see a line of Carrion born creeping along one

branch, ready to storm a Dendran stronghold. This bunker is more than just a wicker nest but has wooden boards and appears to be embedded in the trunk itself. They're not really in my way, but what the hell, I'm pretty sure I have good reason to hate those fuckers after Igraine ordered my rape and torture.

I flip my rifle over to three shot bursts and pepper the Carrion born. It's comically easy. They fire back at me, but the buckshot spreads too quickly. Hell, even if I was in range, right now everything but my head is bulletproof.

They back away, staying out of my line of sight.

I load another clip and switch back to single shot.

My effect on the battle is sudden and massive. The limited range of the bows and shotguns means that each nest, whether held by treemen or Carrion born, could keep their heads up to spot and repel an attack. Not so now. With my extended range, the Carrion Soldiers are forced to stay under cover at all times. This gives the Treemen time and opportunity to occupy branches and storm their nests.

I move to the bridge I want, eyes on the sky.

I'm pretty sure the Icanitzu and the flight I'd faced earlier are in the next tree.

"Remember me, assholes?" I whisper.

Without caution, I begin to jog across the bridge. I can't let Fabian win this race.

"Sir!" A voice calls from behind me. "We're with you!"

I'm already halfway across the bridge. I look back and see them, a troop of frightened treemen, most of them missing their wicker helms.

"The hell do you want to follow me for?" I call back.

On a scale from one to the god damned wrong thing to say—they suddenly seem terrified. The ones in the back look around themselves nervously, searching for more devils.

I've been free for ten minutes and I already have puppies. "Alright, but you can only help me with the next tree. After that, I'm on my own."

I realize fighting is about the only area where I've met the infidels' expectations. There has to be some reason why I can do this so well, and yet, can't seem to do anything else right.

What was it Q told me? "You are not your enemy, and the quicker you realize that, the better off you'll be."

Or something like that.

I catch a glimpse of Fabian and his crew, my son in tow, through the branches of a neighboring tree. I'm moving parallel with them, which is good, because if I'm right about which tree they're taking my son to, they're going to have to cross my path.

Behind me, my dozen or so followers have caught up. I lead them fearlessly across the remainder of the bridge.

Again, I pick my shots carefully. I can hit enemies in this tree, certainly, and some of the ones in the tree beyond it. I do so carefully, rarely striking more than one man per nest, making sure they stay down. And that seems to be enough. All around me, the battle turns.

Hell can't withstand me.

I'm still tracking Fabian and my son. They're making good time through their trees. His white-cloaked soldiers also have rifles, so they're probably having a similar effect on their battle. There's a broad walkway complete with a boarded floor which runs like a road through a series of tightknit trees perpendicular to my path. The treemen called the structure something special. The longbridge. I assume that's where Fabian and his boys will cross to the Safe Tree.

My cadre has left me, thank God, and is storming some Carrion born held nest to save civilians. The tree ahead is full of devils, not Carrion born. I trot across the bridge toward it. As I step onto a branch, I hear the leathery flap of wings.

I turn to see the two survivors of the flight I'd fought earlier.

"I missed you fuckers."

I raise my rifle.

The second great explosion rocks the chamber.

The concussion of the blast hits me a split second before a wave of dirt and gravel. The branch beneath me sways, and I drop to one knee to keep my balance. I hear the pop of distant bridges and the cries of men and dyitzu toppling into the abyss. Somewhere a woman is crying. A baby, perhaps the baby used against my son in the trial, gives out a long wail.

The air is again so thick with dust that I can barely see. Clouds of it billow through the branches. Silt and stone sift down through the upside down canopies.

A dead man falls past me.

It's worse for the flying devils. The dezendyitzu clutches a branch, stone shrapnel in one eye. Unlucky fucker. That could have easily been me.

I sling the M-16 behind my back and draw the Old Lady. Even from where it clings, the thing reaches out a clawed hand as if to attack me. I take a couple unsteady steps toward it and blast its face off at point blank range. Even while dead, it hangs onto the branches. Through the thickened haze, I see one of its cousins, flapping oddly in the air. Its equilibrium must be off. I fire a blast. It gets its wings up as a shield in time, but the action costs it altitude. It struggles back into the air, slamming into a trunk. I take the opportunity to fire again.

This time I score a hit in the dezen's side. It launches off the tremendous tree, sailing straight at me. I fire another blast. Again, the dezen shields but that interrupts its swoop and it soars underneath me. It gains altitude on the far side as I load more shells.

The Icanitzu, black eyes glinting, steps toward me out of the mist, its backward jointed legs a little wobbly.

The dezendyitzu hurls fire at me, but its equilibrium must not be completely back yet because I don't even have to dodge. I pop off another couple shots to keep the thing plummeting. Then I sheath the Old Lady and draw the gladius from my pack.

The Icanitzu must recognize the weapon because it launches off the branch and dives into the abyss.

Damn.

I was really looking forward to killing that one. The

dezendyitzu follows its leader.

The mist isn't clearing, so I just have to guess that Fabian is still on course to get my son to the Safe Tree.

I feel a breeze though, for what that's worth.

Again the world around me is a hellacious, grey wonderland. Distant spheres of fire illuminate baubles of fog on their routes through the chamber, reminding me strangely of the bolts of energy I'd seen traveling through the Erebus. The calls and cries of battle seem more sporadic now. It's hard to kill people you can't see. This certainly cancels the effectiveness I gained from having the M-16, but maybe it's good for Dendra in general.

I traverse the landings and come to a short bridge. One guardrail is down, but it looks like it can hold my weight.

Perhaps the most unlucky dyitzu in the labyrinth happens to be crossing over from the other side. A blast from the Old Lady sends it tumbling.

I slide in a replacement shell as the breeze picks up force, swirling the haze about. I cross and leave the shaky bridge quickly, climbing up to the roots of the tree. The mist seems to dissipate as I rise, and I entertain the hope of catching a glimpse of my son.

A wicker home rests in the crook of one of the top branches. I see a young woman through an open door, her eyes afire, kneeling in the center of her home. She puts a finger to her lips, signaling for me to be quiet.

She's armed with the broken shaft of an arrow. It's something, I guess. The point is bloody, so she seems to have used it already.

Ducking under the low wicker archway, I enter, stepping across the creaking boards as quietly as I can.

I stand on a pile of skins and blankets which must have been her bed and look out through her window toward where I expect Fabian to be. The woman steps up next to me, also surveying the chamber.

The line of trees Fabian had traveled along is visible, certainly, but barely. The branches and leaves all appear grey through the turbulent mists. But over there, where the explosion occurred, the air is clearer. Another fresh cave gapes open along the edge of Dendra's chamber. Dyitzu line it, looking for targets.

Then I see Callodax. He's mounted on the back of a giant silverleg spider.

He can control devils.

"He's betrayed us," the woman says, having apparently spotted the infused at the same time as me.

I turn to her. "You saw me in the trial? You know who I am?"

"Yes," she says.

"And you know where the Wicker Tree is?"

"Of course."

"I need you to go and save the other infidels. Do you understand?"

She shakes her head. "No, infidel, you brought this

upon us."

She's probably right about that. "Okay, then you better make for an exit. I'm not sure if Dendra controls any of them, but that's your only shot."

She cocks her head to one side. "Why not you? Why don't you save your friends?"

Because I have to save my son.

Callodax's silverleg mount is climbing the wreckage of the far wall. Then it jumps onto a branch. He wants my son. This entire attack is about Callodax getting my son—or possibly me—either way, Callodax must die.

I point to the infused. "I'll make you a deal. I'll try and kill that thing, and you try to rescue my friends."

She thinks about this. "Okay."

Once more into the breach.

Callodax's eight-legged mount thrashes about itself, impaling a pair of fleeing women. Callodax himself has a rifle, which triggers something in my mind. Could it be this easy? If Callodax can touch old world substances, then he can be shot.

I just need to get to a good vantage point. With a long, loping run, I traverse the bridge to the next tree. The millions of years my ancient ancestors spent in African canopies pays dividends now. I leap from branch to branch, and when they are too far apart, I find handholds in the trunk's rough grey bark.

My target is a sap drawing station near the roots above me.

Callodax is only a tree away from me now, on one of the larger platforms which helps support the longbridge. Icanitzu and dezendyitzu surround the bastard, hurling fire and lending their wings to protect him. The infused and his cohorts are cutting their way through a mass of women and children.

Josh had thought the civilians were going to be taken to the Safe Tree, but these people must not have had time to make it to their sanctuary. Something in my soul twangs like a broken string as I watch a silverleg spiderleg impale a helpless boy. Guards are rushing in even now, trying to make some space for their unarmed citizens to flee, but the treemen are getting the worst of it. Their arrows don't seem strong enough to pierce the dezens' wings. Hell, my bullets weren't even powerful enough earlier.

The good news is, though, that at this distance, the dezendyitzu will not know to shield against my fire.

I crest the edge of the small platform and unsling my M-16. I lay down, shouldering my rifle. The fact the infused is a tree away and riding on the back of a twitchy arachnid isn't going to make my job any easier.

Desperate treemen usher their women and children across the platform, often paying for the struggle with their lives.

There's a branchwall which runs across the platform. Two men are at the base helping the fleeing line of often wounded civilians over it. From where I sit,

I can see on both sides of the wall. On Callodax's side are the demons and the fighting treemen. On the far side they're collecting the survivors.

There's a pair of kids running away, though guards call out fiercely after them. They're trying to make it to the longbridge. A dezendyitzu sweeps down and grabs one. The other is caught by an Icanitzu. Jesus Christ.

I hear the high-pitched scream of what must be a mother as her child is borne away.

I've got you, little guy. Just hang on.

As I steady my aim, I notice the dezendyitzu releasing its child, dropping the poor kid into the mists. Too late. I turn back to Callodax.

Even as I fire, Callodax turns toward me.

His head jerks back, like he was bitten by a horsefly. Holy fuck, please tell me he didn't dodge my bullet. I fire again, but this time it's his arm that twitches.

I am hitting him, my bullets just aren't doing any damage.

He's staring right at me. Fuck.

Two treemen hurl spears at the beast he rides. One bounces off the spider's exoskeleton. The other buries itself in the arachnid's side. The treemen aren't cut out for this. Armed with arrows and spears, they can hold a nest—but there, on the open platform, exposed to the swooping devils and the dyitzu fire, they don't stand a chance.

But I don't care about them, right? I'm just here for my son.

I need to get moving again. With all this fighting at the branchwall, Fabian isn't going to be able to use the longbridge to get to the Safe Tree. What route will he take?

I can backtrack and get there via the Prima Tree.

Come on, Cris. There's nothing you can do here. Nothing. You saw that your bullets can't affect the thing.

But I don't move.

I can't make myself move.

Instead, I steady my breathing and drop a dyitzu, and then another. And another.

The battle is lost, but I can't abandon helpless children.

Please, Cris. You don't care about them. Your son is on the line here. Remember those bastard tikes that threw rocks at you in Maylay Beighlay? That's all these kids are. They're monsters, just like every other human being. Just like the Nazis. Like the murderers and the thieves.

Just like me.

I fire again, missing. I switch clips.

I'm just wasting ammo. My efforts aren't going to be enough. I see that now. The treemen are fleeing already. I take out a few of the devils in pursuit, dropping one dyitzu even as it forms a fireball.

The treemen are cresting the branchwall as they flee, many of them dying as they cross to the safe side. I fire a few three shot bursts, forcing some of the devils to take cover.

One of the retreating treemen should be ushering the children away. Others should hold the branchwall in a heroic last stand as the children escape along the longbridge. But that's not happening.

If Cid were in control of the battle, that's what would be happening.

But then I see help coming, treemen running along the longbridge from the Safe Tree. They're armed with guns, too, not just bows! In their midst is a man clad in black.

Amirani.

And, as if they are my own children he's coming to save, my heart soars to see him.

I fire more and reload. Only two clips left. I'll need to get closer to help.

I descend, looking for a good place to cross.

Amirani and his men make one wave, while Callodax and his devils make another. They meet at the branchwall, and for a moment I can't see which side will crest over the other.

Reports of gunfire fill Dendra's chamber. Amirani, also armed with an M-16, empties a couple of clips. He knows some strategy which is fucking up the dezendyitzu. For whatever reason they can't seem to get their wings up in time like mine did.

I make it to a bridge which crosses over to that platform.

Alright, Amirani, hold on. I'm on my way . . . not that I have a fucking clue what I'm going to do when I get there.

Some dezens take notice of me and release a few volleys of fire as I approach. There's almost nowhere to dodge on the bridge, so I duck.

The wave passes mostly overhead, but a few burst on the guardrail vines and the fire splashes on me. As before, the fire dies on the infidel armor, but one searing droplet burns painfully on the back of my hand. I move forward, shaking the droplet off, but stop cold as I hear the popping of vines.

Oh shit, my bridge is about to go.

I drop to the braided floor and wrap my legs around it. More dyitzu fire is coming.

It gives.

Oh, Lucifer, what the fuck did I ever do to you?

My stomach is in my chest as I and my bridge plummet down past the branches, dyitzu fireballs passing all around me.

Then, with a sudden jerk, the vine pulls taut and my momentum forces me downward toward the bridge's singed end. My legs snap through two pairs of supports for the guardrail before I get caught on the third.

I'm swinging, like some infidel Tarzan, through the upside down Hellforest.

And I'm heading for a trunk.

But then I'm in the thick of the canopy, leaves the size of people grabbing at me and my bridge. Another branch, somewhat perpendicular to my path, catches the vine above me, and I'm swinging up.

For a split second I'm weightless, then the vine swings backward.

I don't wait for it to stop completely before I start climbing.

My adrenaline fueled limbs power me up the vine. It's like I'm Q or something.

I arrive at the platform and there's a cheer from the treemen. I duck a fireball and draw my gladius, hoping to catch sight of what caused the treemen's celebratory call. They're looking at me.

Oh, they're cheering for me.

And of course they are.

They don't know I'm not fully trained and emotionally unstable. They don't know I've been defiled. Instead, they think I'm here to fight for them. To protect them and their children from demons.

Hell, maybe I even am.

I lay about me with the ancient-forged sword, hacking and stabbing and ducking and turning, making my way to the branchwall as friendly arrows and bullets fell the devils which get too close. The platform seems larger when you're standing on it, and uneven planks make each running step treacherous. Dyitzu take cover in the broken gaps between the planks, rising and hurling their missiles before dropping down again to stay out of the defenders' fire. The branchwall rises up above me, perhaps ten feet tall, a perfect obstacle to the devils' progress. As I mount it, I see Amirani facing off against Callodax. Amirani, like myself, stands at the apex of the wall, his infidel sword in his left hand, batting away at the sudden jabs of the six foot silverleg blades as he fires his M-16, one handed, with his right. He's shooting at the thing's eyes, which seems smart.

Callodax's spider mount has its rear legs dug into the platform. Its middle legs rake at the branchwall as it strikes with its upper limbs.

Callodax's rifle discharges, but of course, the bullet does nothing to Amirani's infidel armor. I sheath my gladius as I run to them, avoiding fireballs and drawing the Old Lady. The spider is using three of its bladed legs to jab at Amirani. I take aim at where the silver meets the natural part of the spider. The end of the blade-leg seems almost like a sewing needle, and I can see the insectine tendon which threads through it. I blast away, green ichor erupting from where the shot pierces the exoskeleton around the joint.

Callodax reaches down to the spear stuck in the spider's side and tugs it free. Then he adds it to the weapons attacking Amirani. The infused bastard is quick, but Amirani stays clear, moving away from me along the branchwall. It takes two more blasts at the joint before the silver blade falls free.

Callodax and his mount turn their back to me and give chase to Amirani, running beside him along the branchwall, the points of the seven remaining legs throwing up wood and plant matter into the air. I give pursuit, loading more shells as I dodge around fighting treemen.

Amirani turns on a dime, slipping the spear thrust of the infused, burying his sword into the face of the giant silverleg.

Before Callodax strikes again, the Infidel Friend darts out, goo and bits of spider eyes trailing off his sword with the consistency and color of infected phlegm. The spider, perhaps blinded, charges on for a second, slower to stop than Amirani.

I hear the telltale whistle.

When I look back to Amirani, I see him diving

behind the branchwall. I take his cue and jump down, landing beside him.

He acknowledges me with a nod at the exact instant that the explosion goes off. Fire, shrapnel, and spider guts erupt from behind the wall as I feel the boards beneath me tremble. Beside me I can see the wicker hut where the children have been gathered. Two heroic treemen make their stand, fending off an Icanitzu with their spears.

Through the wicker wall I see Fabian's wife, huddling with another pair of women amidst the kids. For the first time I see the women civilians through infidel eyes. Why aren't they fighting? How could they trust these men around them to ensure their safety?

And worse, what fucked up society poisons everyone's minds so badly that not even Hell can shake off the brainwashing?

I want Amirani to give me orders, to tell me something that will make sense of the mess, but instead he leaps back up to the branchwall, expecting me to be what I am not. Or perhaps trusting I can become what I so badly need to be.

I follow him onto the branchwall using a knot to propel me upward. My balance does not fail me as I come to the top.

The spider is below us, still alive, dangling from the edge of the platform with two of its bladed legs buried into the burnt wood. Callodax, strapped to his saddle, is struggling to free himself.

Amirani hacks at one leg, and I level the Old Lady at the other. I hold my trigger down and pump out five shells, one a slug and the other four buckshot. Both legs detach and the spider, Callodax and all, plunges down into the canopied mists below. Icanitzu and dezendyitzu dive over the ledge after them.

I hope somewhere far below those mists, when Callodax hits bottom, the spider lands on him.

Again the treemen cheer.

"Is Cid out?" Amirani yells, ducking a dyitzu fireball.

"No!" I respond. "I sent someone—"

"I'll ensure she's free. Hold the platform. Keep the kids safe."

I see Fabian and his men heading our way along the longbridge. If I hold this place for just a little while, and if Fabian has to make it to the Safe tree, my son will come to me. For once, being this thing, this infidel, and being Cris, are perfectly aligned.

There is nothing so restorative to a warrior's soul than purity of purpose.

Amirani eludes a few fireballs as he heads down the platform. I see a couple of Icanitzu returning, fluttering back up from where they'd dived fruitlessly after Callodax.

"Stay at the wall!" I yell to the treemen. "We'll rush the devils when Fabian arrives to make sure he can get to safety."

For some reason they obey me. Somehow I knew they would. I'm pretty sure when Fabian gets here, he's going to want to kill me, but that shit won't fly when I'm leading Dendra's soldiers.

That means Fabian and I are on the same side right now. Of all the fucked up things . . .

We charge down from the wall as Fabian, his men and my son arrive. The dyitzu, leaderless and caught off guard by our sudden willingness to engage them, do not react well. To my right a few treemen spear an Icanitzu. AK-47 blasts from Fabian's six white-cloaked guards take out a few returning dezendyitzu from the sky.

I fell a dyitzu on my way to Fabian.

The dyitzu hiding in the gaps between planks are forced to find new cover as we advance. They flee across the ruined and burning boards, diving off the edge of the platform and onto the supporting branches.

Fabian's got Aiden's hands tied behind his back,

bastard. My boy's black eyes are completely expressionless, his face set in something like the wight equivalent of an infidel's stoicism.

Is he glad to see me?

"This way!" I shout to Fabian and his men, and then louder, so the rest of the treemen can hear me. "Back to the wall."

My men lay down a little extra fire at the dyitzu's new positions and begin an orderly retreat.

I keep my eyes on the dyitzu as I usher Fabian and his soldiers back across the body littered platform. "When was the last time you talked to the Tree Lord?" I shout over the sounds of the remaining combat.

"At the beginning!" one of Fabian's men answers. "We were ordered to get the wights and deliver them to Callodax in exchange for help in this fight."

Wights? As in plural? What happened to Durgan?

Fabian gives his man a sharp look, but then speaks up himself. "At the time we didn't know Callodax was the one attacking."

"Makes sense," I say. "Down everyone!" A pair of fireballs floats over us. "When the blast knocked out my bars, I immediately went to the Tree Lord. He said you guys had left a while before. He's pissed as hell right now."

Fabians snorts. "Damn right."

Lying to Fabian makes me feel better about fighting alongside him, for some reason.

I leap up, mounting the branchwall with two giant steps.

"Back over the wall!" I shout to the soldiers. "Covering fire!" Then I turn and offer a hand to Fabian and his men. "He said he wants Callodax dead. And he doesn't want the wights anywhere near them."

Fabian is first. I crouch low and strain with my legs to power the huge man up.

He's suspicious, but his men aren't. Fabian, in this case, has the right of it, but I can't help but feel like this means his guys are better people. The next man is much easier to help up.

"The Tree Lord gave me permission to fight in the battle," I say.

This eases Fabian, not because it makes the story any more believable, I'm guessing, but because my lie makes it sound like Dendra's power structure is still intact. I look back to the Prima Tree. Hell, it's entirely possible that the Tree Lord's already dead.

With my gladius, I cut Aiden's bonds as if it's the most normal thing a person can be doing. Fabian's eyes bulge.

"Infidel," one man shouts to me, "look!"

My cockles warm at the realization that he reported to me rather than Fabian, but the sensation doesn't last.

A stream of pigmaditz are soaring across the chamber, and they're taking a ninety-degree turn right toward us.

I look back to Fabian. "The Tree Lord said keeping the wights away from Callodax was priority number one. Get those kids," I point to the nursery, "and your wife to the Safe Tree. I'll hold the imps, if they can be held."

Fabian's nostrils flare, but then he sees his wife and becomes lost looking at her. I guess maybe, deep down, he might actually love her.

"Aiden," I tell my son, "stay with Fabian and stay safe. Try and keep the kids away from the dyitzu."

"Yes, Cris," he responds.

"This way," Fabian orders his men, apparently now on board with my plan.

"We're going to buy the women and children time!" I shout to the treemen, still finding it a little fucked up that Dendra has somehow convinced its women that they aren't fighters. "Hold the line."

My men steel themselves, drawing bows and shouldering rifles and shotguns.

"I'm low on arrows," one wicker-helmed man says.

A chorus of others agree, and a few say they're out.

"Then make sure you have a spear," I answer.

XXVI

I meet the golden horde of pigmaditz with a canister of infidel fire. I mistime it, and the blast goes off below them, but the shockwave does more to scatter the formation than I could have hoped. The first wave hits the wall at a tumble rather than a glide, propelled forward by the blast. Those immediately above the fire fly over us, and those farther back swoop in too low.

The treemen are smarter than me. They duck down behind the branchwall, stabbing up with their spears.

Not me. I'm an idiot.

I stand there, pistol in one hand, gladius in the other, slashing and shooting at the three-foot golden devils.

From that vantage point I see a fresh pack of dyitzu coming down the longbridge. They might have been chasing Fabian.

"We need more fucking arrows," I shout. "Dyitzu coming."

One man is kicking a pigmaditz off the end of his spear. "There's more in the Safe Tree armory."

I take stock of the branchwall. It doesn't look like these pigs are going to be enough to dislodge us.

"Hold the wall!" I cry. "I'll be back with arrows."

A cheer goes up. Fuck me. They really are buying this Cris-is-an-infidel shit. I run, legs pumping, past the nursery and back onto the longbridge.

Fabian is stepping onto the Safe Tree, my son between his men.

"Fabian!" I shout. "Arrows. We need arrows from the armory."

A huge barrage of fireballs roll across the chamber, coming from my right. It looks like a thousand of them. They sweep by, some impacting with the bridge, most tearing above or below it. I keep an eye out to make sure I don't get hit.

This run is going to be more exciting than I thought.

I jump over a puddle of fire.

The barrage keeps coming, but thankfully it's mostly over the longbridge now. The structure is as stable as any in Dendra, but that's not much to brag about. I get more vertigo as the wooden planks bounce beneath my racing feet.

At some point during the fighting, the air had cleared.

I make it to the Safe Tree. I see my son climbing into a giant nest next to Fabian's wife.

Two of Fabian's men are coming back with quivers of arrows.

"Load me up!" I shout.

Fabian is carrying a quiver for me too. "We're headed back to the Prima Tree for orders," he says, putting the quiver around my neck.

Well, they'll find out I lied, but hell, maybe that means I'll get to shoot this son of a bitch.

I hold up my arms and his men sling the quivers on me. I see a Dendran citizen moving along the Prima Tree bridge in a hurry, headed toward us. He's calling for Fabian.

"I'll get back to the branchwall," I say. "We'll secure that tree and start taking them out. With Callodax gone we should be able to finish them off."

Fabian nods.

The longbridge is still in good shape, thank God, but—

Oh fuck.

A wave of fire, like the tremendous barrage I saw earlier, hits the branchwall. The inferno rolls over the defenders, cresting with a spray of fiery droplets.

They're screaming.

One man, burning, drops off the platform and plummets to his death. Pigmaditz are soaring over and through the inferno. And there, above it all, held in the clutches of two Icanitzu, is Callodax.

They let the infused down where the platform meets the longbridge. The conflagration forces the survivors toward him.

Oh fuck.

"Fabian!" someone is shouting.

It's the citizen coming from the Prima Tree.

"What?" Fabian is breathless, his eyes on the blazing branchwall.

"The Tree Lord is dead," he shouts. "He ordered you to kill the wights."

Fabian's men turn to stare at me.

"Aiden, run!" I scream.

Fabian turns quickly and levels his AK-47 as Aiden takes cover in the Safe Tree bunker.

"No, Fabian!" I shout.

He fires off some rounds. I leap at him, forcing the gun upward. He knees at me, and I circle quickly around him.

"Fabian!" I shout again, and wrap up his broad chest with my arms. "Fabian, you can't. He's a wight."

He grunts, fighting my hold. His men grab the quivers slung around my shoulders and try to drag me off.

"Your bullets won't hurt him, Fabian!" I scream. "He's a wight."

Fabian rips out of my hold and shoulders his AK-47.

He'll kill civilians, he'll kill his own—"Fabian! You'll kill your wife."

He freezes. The men tugging at me stop too.

"He's immune to bullets," I say quickly to hammer the point home, "but the women and children aren't, Fabian. You'll only kill them."

He frowns, slowly comprehending, the nostrils of his hooked nose flaring.

I let the quivers on my arms fall off and remove the one from around my neck. "The Tree Lord is dead, Fabian. You've got to get them to safety."

Aiden has made a break for it and is running down the vine bridge to the Prima Tree.

"We should kill him, Fabian," one white-cloaked man says, pointing at me.

Damn, and I thought he was the smart one. I could take a few bullets before they realize they need to shoot for my head, and there's a nest I can duck into . . . but they don't *have* to kill me. No one has ordered them to, so far as they know.

"One second!" I shout.

And just like the Tree Lord had paused and listened to Cid for no fucking reason, they listen to me.

"Callodax is coming!" I say pointing back to the

longbridge. "You know I want my son alive, so you know I've got to stop him. You guys save the children. I'll die fighting Callodax."

Fabian mulls this over while his men watch. "Okay," he says reluctantly, probably considering whether he wants to fight Callodax in my stead. "Get the kids."

How nice of you.

I should probably shoot him right now.

But there Callodax is, his back to me, stepping backward onto the longbridge. Ahead of him, the platform burns, sending small flaming pieces of itself shooting down like falling stars into the mists. Pigmaditz flee the conflagration, taking to the air in all directions, but the dyitzu are shit out of luck.

A dozen surviving treemen are charging Callodax in an attempt to get by him and escape the flames.

Callodax has that fucking latch action rifle. They shoot him with arrows and bullets, but he doesn't care. He just reloads and fires, reloads and fires.

Fabian rushes after my son as his men direct the women and children out of the nest. I just have to trust that Aiden can stay away. Or kill Fabian. Killing him would be nice. I drop to one knee, flipping my M-16 to single shot mode, and take careful aim. Callodax won't fear me. I can't hurt him. I fire a bullet at his rifle. Miss.

Again.

Miss.

Fuck this is hard.

Again.

Got it.

Again.

Yes!

Again.

The smell of the M-16's gunpowder seems strangely sweet for some reason. Or maybe it's burning sinfruit.

He goes to fire his rifle, but no dice. I'd damaged it!

Callodax tosses the rifle aside and picks up a spear.

I draw my gladius, snag my last two canisters of infidel fire, pocket them, and drop my pack.

"Infidel!" a woman's voice calls from behind me.

There they are, women and children, waiting at the Prima Tree's bridge. Why the hell are they still here?

My heart stops.

It's not a planked bridge, so people are only supposed to go across three at a time. Fabian's got them doing ten or so, but they don't even have the first group all the way over.

One girl is lying on her side, and I see a long red bloody line where a blade, probably a silver spider leg, had cut deeply into her thigh.

They'll have to carry her.

But she can die. A thousand of her can die, a million, so long as Aiden lives.

I step up to the longbridge. The last of the treemen

have died. Callodax is already coming. Merciless. Unstoppable.

Or seemingly so. I'd tried shooting him. I could try dropping him into the abyss again, but the Icanitzu would just flying-monkey his ass back up here.

Maybe I need to switch up my tactics and kill the Icanitzu which carry him back up. But there's just one of me.

Or maybe my sword can run him through.

I step onto the longbridge, my boots sounding off against the wooden planks.

Alright, motherfucker, ready or not, here I come.

XXVII

Icanitzu hover over Callodax like a flock of gnats. As a bluff, I point my pistol at them. Infidels occasionally have bullets which can hurt Icanitzu. They appear to buy my threat, hovering in place maybe forty yards back as Callodax approaches. If they get any closer, I'm going to fucking firebomb them.

Callodax has his spear under one arm. He seems remarkably competent with the weapon, which scares me a little. How horribly unfair is this about to be if he's not just an infused Revenant, but a better fighter than I, too.

I'm supposed to lead with my sword hand, but I don't, instead keeping my left shoulder facing Callodax.

Maybe I know what I'm doing. Maybe I'm just used to keeping my power hand back. Who the hell knows?

The bridge sways back and forth.

Delay. I'm supposed to delay him so the others can escape.

"What do you want with my son?" I ask, stopping, and squaring off against Callodax.

He also comes to a halt, his bald head shining with a layer of mist. His black turtleneck is torn in places where bullets and arrows have pierced it, but his body, apparently well-muscled and as pale as a man can be without going wight, is inviolate.

The bald head cocks to one side in an inhuman way. His eyes focus on me oddly, as if he's staring through me. I remember how Callodax could sense me looking at him, even through a one-way mirror. How much information can he glean from me? How much am I giving away?

"You think you can win," he states, his arrogant voice as calm as it was during his trial. "Do you know your blade can't hurt me?"

He better be fucking lying.

"You don't know that," he says, as if reading my reaction, then jabs his spear at me.

I slip it, batting at it with my gun hand as if it were a punch. Big mistake, as I can get my hand cut, but I luck out.

My grip on the hilt of the gladius is tight, probably

too tight. I turn sideways toward Callodax trying to keep my profile as small as possible, my left arm still facing him. Honestly, I have no idea how I'm supposed to use a short sword against a spear.

Callodax appears cautious. He's probably never seen anyone fight like this before, and is trying to figure out the why of it.

In this case, the why of it is that I'm clueless.

He tries a pair of tentative strikes. I back away quickly from the first one, and slip the second—keeping my hand away from the blade this time.

He strikes at my leg, and I switch stances backward to dodge it. He tries again, and I execute the same move.

My heart thunders in my chest. I wish this damn gladius was longer. How the hell am I supposed to get close enough to hit him? And why are the bullets bouncing off of him? I have a theory about that. When a bullet hits a wight, its momentum disappears completely. In this case, Callodax's head is jerking back. The bullets are hitting him, and transferring their momentum to him, but they just aren't doing any damage. Maybe this infidel blade is different, or maybe I just need a lot more force.

He jabs again, and I slip it, dropping my head and torqueing my hips to throw an overhand strike with my sword. He shuffles back out of range easily, and the spear's blade, on retraction, cuts my ear.

His eyes narrow.

He knows. The gig is up. It's clear now that I don't know what I'm doing.

Fuck strategy.

I raise my pistol and fire at his face. He jumps forward at that exact moment, but his thrust is foiled by the sudden whiplash my bullet imparts upon his head. It's only a split second before he recovers, however, and he strikes twice more with measured jabs. Then he swings the spear haft around at my legs. Somehow I avoid the attacks. He tries again with a killer blow aimed at my torso, but I fire four more bullets into his face in quick succession, and that messes with his aim. I twist away, barely escaping his next strike, and I realize that my feet are about to cross. I turn my bad footwork into what would have been a spinning backfist, but with my gladius, the maneuver becomes a sword strike. My technique is perfect, and the torque of my body and the whiplike momentum of the sword at the end of my reach hits him perfectly on the cheek.

His head jerks to one side.

No blood. No effect.

Oh hell.

I run.

When I dare a look over my shoulder, I see he's readied his spear for a throw. And he releases. I try to dive to one side, my boot catching on a board. I fall, the spear flying over my head and burying itself into the bridge. I twist the cap of one infidel canister and jam it between the planks. I sprint, heedless of the bridge's swaying as the whistle begins. It grows in intensity, and I don't bother to turn around when it comes to climax. I grab a guardrail with one hand and a plank with another.

The blast pops the shit out of my ears.

I look back . . . and the bridge splits in two.

Here we go again.

The longbridge shucks boards as it swings. This time I feel elation as the sudden wind blows through my hair. We don't fall nearly as far as I'd feared because the thing is supported by so many branches. The bridge crushes a cluster of leaves as it buries itself into the Safe Tree's lower canopy. I make quick work of climbing up, coming to my feet easily on the Safe Tree's platform. The women and children have completed their escape, and most of them aren't even on the Prima Tree anymore. Fabian's got the larger portion moved onto the tree beyond, and the last of the civilians are crossing after them.

A pair of dezendyitzu rise, carrying Callodax back

out of the mist amidst the ruins of the longbridge. I shoulder my M-16 and take the first one out. The second one, suddenly off balance, is thrown into a spiral. Maybe because it's too disoriented, it doesn't get its wings up to block me.

Callodax falls back into the abyss, a flock of dezendyitzu and Icanitzu following after.

Fucker.

The bridge to the Prima Tree isn't the kind a man should jog across, but I can't be sure my son is going to last much longer, if he's even alive right now.

I better just get him and get out. I can't think of a way to kill Callodax.

I wonder what would happen if he fell all the way to the bottom . . . and how the hell are the devils able to fly down and catch him? That's fucking annoying.

There's a trio of dezen flying in formation below me. They twist about in the air and start firing up. I stop quickly, and their fireballs collide with the vine bridge ahead. Amirani had been able to shoot them without letting them get their wings up in time. Maybe I'm getting the hang of it by accident because I drop the trio with four three shot bursts.

But that doesn't matter, there are dozens more flying my way. I catch sight of Callodax. They've set him down on the platform of the Safe Tree.

This is not going well, and I'm on my last M-16 clip.

I give caution the metaphorical bird and sprint the rest of the way across the bridge. The cage where we'd been held during the trial has been destroyed, and its remains still smolder. The stand where I'd once given testimony is singed and blackened by dyitzu fireballs. Some dyitzu skin-clad civilians are dead near the counterweights, their bodies scattered amidst the wreckage of ruptured bloodwater barrels. Dead white-cloaked men and devils litter the area, the largest grouping of them in a semi-circle around the Paul Bunyan wound. They might have been defending the Prima Tree's kill switch, waiting for the Tree Lord to make it to safety before activating it.

Only the Tree Lord never made it.

The Tree Lord lies face down near the stand, one hand forward as if he'd been trying to crawl away when finished off by dyitzu fire. His back still smolders where the fat, acting like a candle, keeps a small flame alive.

His Jesus beard is still untouched though.

I see Fabian's men on the next tree. Fabian's there too, but he's being careful to stay out of my line of fire. My son apparently used one of those temporary silk bridges to make it up to a burnt out nest. He's firing arrows at the white-cloaked Dendrans but without much in the way of results. Also on that tree is Keith, Harris, Fin, and some Carrion born. Those bastards have the women and children cornered in a separate nest, though two of Fabian's men are defending them.

There is more gunfire.

Well, *one* of Fabian's men.

Fuck, Fabian. Get some priorities.

I look back. Callodax is on the bridge, coming my way at an even, slow pace. This time he's got eleven or twelve dezen's hovering over him. They don't seem to be focused on me, though.

I better find cover, and not just from them. Fabian's got an AK. There's no way I'll be able to cross the bridge to get my son. Well, maybe. I am bulletproof.

There's got to be a better way. I fire at one of the dezen's, dropping it, and duck down for cover by the stand. The dezens return fire en masse. Fire peppers the tree, hitting the bridge, the platform, some of the dead bodies, and the bloodwater barrels' counterweights.

They must not have seen me before I ducked down.

I know now what I have to do. So much for good Cris. So much for purity of purpose.

"Keith!" I shout.

I come out of my crouch like I'm going to shoot, but I don't.

"I won't stop, Cris!" he calls back from behind a branch. "The kiddies are going to die."

"I don't give a fuck!"

There is a pause, and a little more gunfire rattles off in the distance.

"Okay, I'm listening," Keith calls back.

Callodax isn't rushing. Maybe I should use my last

canister to take out that bridge too.

I shout, "I can kill Callodax, Keith. Do you believe me?"

Fireballs are screaming my way. I drop back down behind the stand. Flaming blasts of liquid rocket up into the sky all around me, droplets coming down like rain. I scoot quickly to one side.

I fire again as the dezens begin to fly forward. Another drops, and that keeps the rest from advancing.

"I do, Godslayer." Keith's call comes back.

"Kill Fabian. And his men. Save my son. I'll free you from Callodax as payment."

There is a moment of pause. The heat of the burning stand is making me sweat in my Icanitzu skin armor.

Fin and Harris, Keith, and the two Carrion born all look to each other.

Keith guns down the Carrion born. "On it," he shouts.

"You'd side with Keith!" Fabian yells at me. "Traitor!"

I shrug the insult off. I'm not sure if I can muster up much guilt for that one. The gunfire on Fabian's tree intensifies as Keith's men start trading shots with Fabian.

Strangely, I feel like laughing. Keith has chased me without fail through the most dangerous parts of Hell. He captured me and drug me to Tintagel. The idea that

Fabian has to deal with that level of bullshit is exciting to me.

Alright, Callodax. I'm all yours.

I step out from my burning cover.

Using the rest of my remaining clip, I drop a single dezendyitzu brave enough to separate from his pack.

Callodax walks at a slasher villain's pace across the narrow bridge, his gait not effected by the swaying. I wonder if that preternatural balance comes from his host, or if it is a result of training, or if it is a property of the soul which inhabits his body.

The fireballs from the distant, more cowardly dezens come thick and fast, but I'm able to avoid them with some minimalistic movements. In the beginning of the battle, it was hard to keep track of all the curving dezen fireballs, but now they seem very predictable.

I draw the Old Lady as another of their number grows bold and pepper it with some shot—enough to bother it, but not enough to kill it. The dezen whirls around in the air, loath to get closer, and moves back in line with its hovering pack.

I make sure the Old Lady is fully loaded, sliding shells into her.

Callodax is at the thirty foot mark. If I'm going to drop this bridge, it's got to be now.

I guess I'm not.

I take aim at one of the next few approaching dezen, it shields itself, and I keep tracking it until it drops out of view. Then I point at another. It drops as well, but as quickly as I can manage, I take aim at the third and fire immediately. The blast bloodies its right shoulder and it begins a downward spiral.

I backpedal toward the counterweights. The canopy is thick and provides me with a good amount of cover. Fireballs from both the brave and cowardly dezens impact with the branches and leaves, sending splashes of multicolored fire across my path. Some of the flaming liquid runs down the leaves even as water might, a path of burnt plant matter left in its wake.

The smell is pungent and bitter.

A dezen finds a gap to get a good shot at me, but my ammunition flies straighter and faster. Its face jerks back with the impact of the buckshot, and its wings lose rigidity. Like a rock, it plummets downward.

Callodax is following me, moving along the branch.

I bet he thinks he'll have me cornered where the branch ends, but he won't because I'll jump onto one of the counterweights. I slide in another shell.

All the remaining dezen are hesitant, now, and I hope that holds. I've got enough to worry about with Callodax and all the pools of fire they've left around me.

Callodax doesn't have a spear this time, thank God. He steps over a leaf's stem as I sheath the Old Lady. It's all about luck from this point on.

I pick up one of the silk-ended temporary bridges.

Come what may.

He's twenty feet from me. Ten feet.

I ready my jump.

Callodax's bald head gleams with the green light of the leaves and the purple light of some still burning dezendyitzu fire. I leap, landing easily on the lower of the two counterweights. It shifts a little from my momentum, its supporting chain links straining as it clunks into its sister weight. I step around the chain and lean back into that second stone mass. I can climb up onto the sister weight, but it's top lip is six feet up, so I might as well have my back to a wall.

Callodax jumps after me.

I toss one end of the repair bridge where I think he'll land.

His right foot lands in the silk. He swings at me, and I jerk back, stepping around the chain. With a quick lunge, he tries to grab me, but the silk holds him fast to the weight.

Yes! Now all I have to do is disconnect the weight.

Then he reaches for his boot.

Fuck.

Won't work.

I need his actual skin to be stuck, not just his boot.

I redraw the Old Lady and let loose three blasts of buckshot into his face. If nothing else, the muzzle flash bothers him, and it can't be easy to see with your head jerking around like that.

He comes at me again, and I block with the other end of the repair vine.

Gotchya, motherfucker.

I'd like to see one of these Icanitzu carry you now.

I sheath the old lady and wrestle him to the side. I jump forward, trying to stick his arm to the sister counterweight, but he's much stronger than I imagined. With his caught hand, he jerks me back toward him, and I don't dare let go of the vine. He headbutts me in the chest. I feel my breath go out, and he might have cracked a rib. With his hand still trapped in the silk, he punches at me. I block instinctively with my left, and the silk envelops my own hand.

Oh God no.

My heart stops.

I try to pull my hand away, hoping that, for some unimaginable reason, I won't be caught in my own trap.

But I am. My hand is buried, wrist deep, in the sticky substance.

Callodax smiles.

We're now linked, myself and this invincible killer, glued together, hand to hand, both flies in the sticky spider silk—silk strong enough to support a bridge.

It's not fair.

All of this. My whole plan. Everything, ruined by a single mistake.

I throw a push kick in revulsion, trying to get some distance, but I'm beyond fucked. My effort doesn't move him, but pushes me away, and I feel the tendons in my left shoulder straining as the silk keeps me from escaping.

This time when he pulls me forward, I don't fight it. He throws a punch, but my lack of resistance catches him off guard and I pass right by. I dance to the corner of the weight, and only the fact that his boot is stuck keeps him from reaching me.

I can't win.

Now I'm fighting merely not to die, and the hopelessness of that settles into my soul.

He pulls again, and again I go with him, but this time I slam our stuck hands into the side of the sister weight. He's stretched out now, his foot and hand each attached to different weights.

I take a breath.

He pulls back with all his might, and his freakish

strength pulls the sister weight into the one we're standing on. Stone grates on stone as he pulls harder, but the silk won't give, and he can't seem to get his free hand on me.

For the moment, I'm safe . . . well from him.

I see a dezen find its way through a gap in the trees. Damn, I thought I'd scared them all away. It launches some fire at me. I duck the fireball as best I can. It impacts with the sister weight and some of it splashes on my armor. None of the fire, for better or worse, catches on the silk. I draw my pistol with my free hand and drop the dezen out of the sky with a flurry of bullets.

"Igraine and her people," Callodax tells me, "I know what they did to you."

I freeze.

He cocks his head. "I know about Shy. About Melvin. About how they made you play the dog."

Of course he would know. I let the empty pistol fall from my hand. It bounces off the stone and plummets away.

My blood, which had previously been pounding in my ears, runs cold, and I remember that sick feeling in my lower intestines after they'd broken me.

"And I know what they took from you, Godslayer. I know how they took it. That does something to a man, does it not?"

Ash flakes drift in the air. The heat of the remaining

dezen fire, dripping slowly down the sister weight beside me, does nothing to warm my cheek. My back shivers so strongly it nearly locks up, and my neck and teeth and ears hurt.

"Haven't you wondered why the soldiers follow me? Why the Carrion born are in my thrall?" he whispers. "Are you interested in experiencing what I did to them? Are you ready to have that taken from you again?"

My breathing slows as my body begins to shut down. It's over. I truly am trapped, now.

You did your best, Cris.

Had I really not known that things were going to end like this? Had I simply ignored the fact that every torture I'd ever experienced was just preparation for the next, worse thing? After Callodax finishes with me, something even more terrible will be waiting. My lot will become more and more unbearable until there is simply nothing worse in this Hell that can be done to me—and then I'll die and go to a new Hell, a Hell so imagined that there *is* something worse that can be done to me.

That's my future. That's always been my future. Only, until now, I'd played this game in my head where I pretended it would never come.

Well here it is. Today is that day.

I remember the state of mind I'd been in when Cid and Q had fought Domina for me. How I did nothing to help myself. How I just shut down.

This is how Callodax wins. I almost fought him to a draw, but when I bound up his physical weapons, he just used psychological ones instead.

I remember the shame I felt when Q looked at me, alone in the darkness of the infidel sanctuary, and saw me for the wretch I'd become.

Through the leaves I see dyitzu pouring over to the Safe Tree, and that seals off the last inkling of hope I might have had. Even if the dezens stay away, Callodax's friends will get here first.

"And your son," Callodax goes on, his words falling like dried leaves onto my dead mind, "wights are not in any way resistant to that torture. It works on them just the same."

Long, long, long is the breath my lungs take in.

I love my son.

I love him as a human, and as a wight. I've loved him since the first second I saw him, since he cried out as a newborn, his naked skin exposed to the harsh air of a world far, far too cruel for his vulnerable body.

Is his future the same as mine? Is even turning into a wight not enough to protect him from the pain of this place?

The first dyitzu are stepping onto the bridge to the Prima Tree. It looks like they're trying to get a better angle on a few remaining treemen across the gap, but I know they won't be held up for long.

I love you, Aiden. I love you, I love you. You are *not* alone.

Tears blur my vision as my heartbeat picks back up, blood again pounding in my ears, as the cacophony of the song of my own violence drowns out whatever words Callodax says next. And it doesn't matter what you say, Callodax. It doesn't matter what you want, or how many devils you have to help you get it.

You freak, you have no idea what I'm willing to do to keep you away from my son.

"Watch!" I scream, my voice shaking.

He's stopped talking.

I draw my gladius.

Callodax regards the weapon, fearless. And of course he's fearless, the sword can't hurt him.

I swing the blade at my wrist.

The agony of the infidel-forged blade cutting into my flesh and bone is unbearable. My body reacts primally to the wound, flooding my brain with the most intense physical suffering I've ever experienced. My vision is clouded. My heart beats so hard in my chest I think I'll die. I can't breathe.

This is the pain people were meant to have. Not the weird emptiness inside your gut or the shame of having your soul laid bare to your enemy. This pain is purer.

I try to pull away but somehow I'm still caught.

My sight comes back, and I notice I haven't severed my hand completely. Blood flows out from my cut flesh.

I can see torn muscle and half-severed bone. He lunges again, reaching with his free hand for my shoulder. I drop back and use that motion as the backswing for my next strike. I cut deeper into my wrist.

Almost.

Again.

So close.

Again.

Free.

I'm on my knees. It doesn't hurt now. Nothing hurts. I try to stand, but my balance is iffy. Blood keeps pouring. Callodax is reaching for me. God help me, I can't move. His fingers try to claw at my face, but I'm an inch out of his reach. I crawl away, almost falling through the gap between the weights. The dezen's purple fire clings to the stone, slowly dripping as a flaming rain into the abyss.

I put my stump into the fire.

The blood nearly puts out the napalm-like substance, but I watch as the skin browns and curls from the heat. My body is sweating, so much that I feel the water collecting in my boots.

I pull the cauterized arm back, inspecting the wound.

Not quite.

I put my arm back in the fire.

Good.

I pull it out.

I look back at Callodax, and rise.

"Watch," I say between quick breaths.

I feel cold, lightheaded, and peaceful despite the inhuman beating of my heart and my hyperventilation. I don't know what's going on. Am I going into shock? I leap off and fall onto the branch beside the weights. I tumble, come up to my knees, and crawl next to the ladder for the counterweights' levers and pulley. I claw my way to my feet and ascend, one armed. The climb is long.

My legs don't want to work.

My vision is getting dim.

There's a small platform here, just like at one of the sap stations, where the pulley is fixed into the tree.

I pull out the infidel fire and unscrew it, jamming it into the counterweight's pulleys.

I try to do the military descent Cid does on ladders, but slip halfway down, landing hard on the wood. To my right, Callodax struggles against the silk as the whistle reaches its climax.

He looks directly at me, and whatever soul inhabits that body is fucking furious.

The infidel fire goes off, blasting the pulley and severing the top part of the chain.

The counterweights fall, trying to separate, but are held together by the tensile strength of the spider silk and the demonic durability of Callodax's infused muscles. I bet that's going to be an absolute bitch when he lands, even for him. Maybe he'll dislocate something. Maybe he'll even die.

I wave goodbye to him with my stump.

The dyitzu on the bridge stop to look at their falling leader.

Dezendyitzu dive after the stone blocks as the weights tumble down the canopy. Callodax's body catches a branch, and the weights pull him down evenly to either side.

For a moment, he's balanced, but then the branch bends, and he rips away a slew of leaves as he slides off the limb.

Now I need to get to my son and the others and get the hell out of here.

I try to stand, but my balance is gone. My head swims. I push myself up the side of the trunk. For a second, I look at my stump.

Big fucking mistake.

I can feel the pain and nothing else. Again I drop to my knees and I hear some man cry out in agony.

That man is me.

You're a fucking infidel, Cris. Your son needs you. His soul loves you. You've got to help.

I make it to my feet again. The infidel fire fucked the ladder, but there's a bridge that runs up around the trunk as well. It's a ramp with no stairs, which is nice. I'm not really in a stairs mood right now. I make a good attempt at a stumbling jog around the spiral of the trunk. I arrive at the platform. My body feels so fucking cold, though I'm still sweating profusely, and salt is getting in my eyes. I blink the perspiration away and—oh no.

Please no.

God.

The dezen flock is rising slowly out of the mists.

Callodax is still attached to one weight, and he's missing a boot. The dezendyitzu and a few Icanitzu are clustered around him and the stone, their wings flapping madly.

Where the hell did those Icanitzu come from?

Together they are lifting Callodax. Their progress is dismally slow, gaining only inches at a time, but they don't have far to go. There is a branch they're angling to rest him on.

Oh no you don't.

After seeing Callodax, I have no difficulty finding my balance. I walk to the smoldering Tree Lord and kick him over. With my remaining hand I reach down and grab the key. I pull, and the leather cord around his dead neck snaps.

Sorry, Jesus.

I put the cord in my mouth and grip it with my teeth. I draw the Old Lady and cock it one handed, jerking the shotgun up and down by the pump.

I fire at the bamboo bars which protect the Prima Tree's kill switch. The buckshot splinters the wood. I cock the Old Lady again and fire a second shell into the bars when I get within a few feet of it. Grasping the Old Lady by her heated barrel, I swing her like a club to clear the remnants of the bamboo.

I sheath the Old Lady.

The key makes a clicking noise as I push it into the lock. It turns easily.

Somewhere in the tree, I hear infidel machinery turn and hum.

Time to go.

I run with renewed vigor, doing my best to keep my coming state of shock away with what must be pure adrenaline.

Through the cracks in the boards, I see they've set Callodax down on one of the branches.

That's not going to work like you think it will.

A chorus of whistles melds together like an army of sopranos singing their polytonic hatred out unto the world. I hit the bridge at a sprint and don't stop.

The blasts go off in quick succession, echoing out across the chamber.

Keith is on the far side of the bridge.

Aiden is there too.

The pair of them, my mortal enemies, a man of the Order and my bewighted son, catch me as I collapse. Harris and Fin take up watch around us, shotguns at the ready. I hear some shouting.

"Stand down," Keith yells at someone. "We only

had beef with Fabian. We're withdrawing. Save your fight for the devils." I hear his whisper. "I've got you, Godslayer."

Then I feel a kiss on my forehead.

Oh, the company I keep.

Another set of explosions boom in sudden, even bursts, each wave occurring about a second apart. It's all I can do to turn my head and look.

One by one, the roots of the Prima Tree erupt in fire and dust and smoke. A hail of stones and dirt issue from each blast, and a slow rain of silt begins. That rain, a halo, descends, forming a nearly opaque cylinder, slowly spreading down around the tree as the demolition continues, obscuring all but the outermost branches. I hear the ripping roots above even the concussions of the blasts. And then, as if it were only tentatively obeying the laws of gravity, the Prima Tree begins its slow fall.

The dezendyitzu and Icanitzu flee the circle of grit and dust, spreading out in all directions like cockroaches faced with an unexpected light. The devils are screaming, perhaps afraid for their own lives, or perhaps feeling some other demonic emotion.

Someone else, a human, is screaming bloody murder. For a second I'm worried that it's me, but the voice is too feminine.

The dust begins to settle over me, but I cannot feel it. I only know it's there because it's getting dark.

They've laid me down against the wall of some corridor somewhere. The smell of trees and leaves and fire is still in my nostrils, but we're not in Dendra. Dim shapes surround me, but their faces are the faces of my friends.

Thank God. If I ended up back in Keith's custody, I think I'd have just gone ahead and gotten the stilling.

"He's awake," Q says.

"My son?" I ask.

"He's safe, with us." Cid's voice answers.

"Is Callodax dead?"

I feel a hand against my forehead. "No fucking clue," Cid says. "We need to get word to Ares or Endymion or someone to come check, just in case."

"The Infidel himself?"

I'm able to focus enough to see Cid's face.

"No," she answers. "He's *way* too far out. But it needs to be an infidel we can trust has the power to kill it."

I look to the stone ceiling. It feels nice to be in the wilds again. I see Amirani by an exit, keeping watch. I'm glad he's come with us.

"What if Callodax is following us?" Neb asks.

Cid stands. "Then he'll follow us right to Endymion or Ares. That'd be good."

Q shrugs. "If worst comes to worst, we can always just throw Cris at him again, and see what happens."

I smile.

Cid had settled us down in a series of rooms along the Northern Lethe. She'd said there were places along the river where it's safe to camp, and that this place is one of them.

I'd offered to take watch, not because I was well enough to, but because I need to be alone—badly. Oh so very badly.

She wouldn't let me take watch, but there's a room by the river whose only exit leads back to camp, so it's safe. We bathed in it, and I've returned here now to be by myself.

Though I'm as tired as I've ever been, I can't seem to sleep.

My mind won't stop working. It's like it realizes there is something missing, and it wants to keep thinking until my hand regrows.

I sit on a boulder and try to wait out my thoughts.

Hell heals all wounds, thank God. Would I have chopped off my hand if it wouldn't regrow?

Maybe.

I feel miserable.

Must be the shock.

Or maybe it's that I killed half of Hell and, despite all that, my son is still a wight.

I think of the room in Maylay Beighlay—as the river rushes by—where Myla died. Where the workers—the river is quite interesting. It cuts the room in two, but it's hardly straight. Usually the rivers in Architect-touched rooms have squared banks, but this one is more natural, as if it's allowed to have its way with the bricked stone around it.

The chamber's ceiling isn't very high. I could jump and touch it, I think. I scratch my cheek with my remaining hand.

I can tell my body wants to cry again.

Really? Now? Isn't it all over? I won, God damn it.

But these tears are different. I can't stop them. I try, but they come anyway—little bitch that I am.

Cid wouldn't cry.

I wait for the tears to pass, but they don't. I do my best to keep them quiet, but I can't.

Instead I collapse to the ground and curl into a ball.

I cover my face with my arms, fighting to keep the ugly feeling in, but the emotion bleeds out anyway. My chest and abdomen clench in sudden even bursts as my soul tries to do something, anything, to express itself. But what this agony is, why it's come or why it won't go, I don't know.

I hear light steps.

And Cid is here, my angel, her arms wrapping around me. "It's okay, lover."

Something is broken inside me. I've been such a little shit in the last month or so, and I've had plenty of time to get used to myself crying—but now something isn't right. There is something *wrong* with me. Something that won't be fixed from another session with Cid or even after a decade of relative safety. Crying usually gives me some release, but these aren't those kind of tears.

I'm not crying to express grief. There's too much of it for that. I'm crying for help because I can't do this on my own.

"What's wrong with me?" My words shake like a little boy's.

"I'm sorry, Cris," she whispers.

Cid pulls me up in her arms. I remain mostly curled up, my hip on the stone and my back on her chest. Her hair falls across my face, damp hair, because she's crying too. Softer tears than mine. Tears of empathy. Tears that don't make her sob, or hate, or act irrationally. Infidel tears.

Her lips touch the back of my head. "This time it's my fault."

But she's lying. I hurt so much.

So much.

"No," I say. "My son. I was raped, I . . ."

"I know why you're crying, Cris."

"I'm broken. My son. My—"

"It's not those things, lover," she says. "This is different."

I turn my head and look up through her trusses of black hair.

"You're crying because you know. Because you understand what the labyrinth is really about. You know what it wants from you, and what it will someday get. You know it will get these things from those you love as well. From me, and from your son.

"But you'll cry again, someday. You'll cry because you didn't save Dendra. You'll cry because you brought on their destruction. You'll cry because you chose your son over an entire village. You'll cry because you initiated the continued torture of so many people. You'll cry because you know you're responsible for all that, and you care about people, Cris. Some of those tears will be my fault, because I'm the one teaching you to care."

"I hate myself, Cid." Because I betrayed her at

every turn. Because I lied and wheedled and used every tool she'd given me to get what I want, consequences be damned. Because . . .

Now I'm seeing myself clearly, past all the little tricks people use to make themselves think they are good. Oh, God. No wonder Earth was such a mess. No wonder there were wars and hate up there. No one taught us how to see ourselves clearly, and who would want to if they knew what evil thing lay underneath the webs of convenient lies our subconsciouses whisper into our gullible ears?

But Cid had taught me other things about people too. Of course I'd do what I did. I'm human. I'm biased. I used lies to meld an unfriendly reality with the idea that I was a worthwhile person.

I'd had this expectation of myself, that I'd be a rational creature, a thing with a mind of an angel that can do what is right. That cares what is right. That *is* what is right.

But rational is not what I am. It's not what people are.

We are despicable self-deceivers.

But not Cid.

Cid very nearly has that angel mind. She wasn't born with it, that I know. She must have fought like hell to get it, facing difficult truths which the rest of us turn away from.

When I pretended I was good, I was cheapening

her effort. Her ungodly effort.

Maybe we humans can be beautiful after all.

I have never admired anyone as much as I admire her now. Her face, so familiar to me, covered in tears and wet hair, etched with an almost superhuman concern—it fits somehow. There's a part of my mind which expects her blue-green eyes. That knows the curve of her chin and the shape of her slightly upturned nose. I know each of the muscles in her cheeks and how they play across her delicate features. I know each expression she has and which emotion brings them.

Her battle against her own nature to become this thing, this paragon, this archetype, this warrior, this . . . this infidel—it must have been a crusade the likes of which I've never seen. I want that fight. It must be tougher than my fight with Callodax, but I want it. I want to stand on that hill for another. I want to reach back down and help everyone else like she helps me. I want this. Because right now, now that I've seen the truth about myself, the other alternative is to be *this* miserable.

I never knew, in all my life, that I cared this much about being a good person. What does it say about me that I had this buried within my soul? How many others do? Are there those that don't? Is it Cid that drew this out of me? Or Q? Or my son? Or God? Or the Devil?

Or me.

I sit up. "I'm ready."

She smiles. "Where should it go?"

Hers is on her hand, on her palm. Q's is on his right shoulder.

"On my palm," I say. "Like yours, because you're bringing me across."

She smiles. "I'll get the rustrock."

Her tears are gone when she returns. She sits down cross-legged beside me, a vial in one hand. She draws her infidel dagger with the other.

"I love you, Cris," she says.

I no longer feel like infidel love is cheap. Now it seems to me that the other kind of love is selfish.

"I love you, too."

She coats the blade with a solution of rust rock.

I hold out my hand. She sits up on her knees, like a Japanese warrior, her hair spilling in front of her eyes. She cuts a delicate tracery of lines into my skin. It doesn't hurt because, compared with the agony of chopping off my own hand, this kind of pain is a distant, whistling breeze.

"It is upon your soul that I place this mark," she whispers, "that you might carry the light. It is incumbent upon you to extract the knowledge of Hell's workings from her very stones. To draw from yourself and others the knowledge of our own natures. To continually learn and grow in pursuit of *arete*. That you might use these devices, no matter how painful they are to behold and acquire, to fight. That you might be a part of conquering the labyrinth. That you might make Hell Eden.

"You are *Jus Sanguinis*, and it is by my blood that you are made one with us."

Then she puts her dagger aside and wraps my hand.

My heart is pounding, and it makes my stub itch.

I feel like I have transformed, but I know this isn't quite true. I have only decided to change. The hard work is in front of me.

She ties off the bandage and looks into my eyes. "When you become an infidel, you are often given a name. You might use it right away, or you might not. You might wait until a day comes when all that you have known has passed away, when you are a stranger surrounded by strangers. This happens to some of us, you know, when we outlast our loved ones. Then you can pick up that mantle if you so choose.

"I give you the name of Diomedes, because you are fool enough to fight gods, and strong enough and lucky enough to win."

And then she pulls me close to her chest, and holds me tight. "I love you. I love you. Cris, Diomedes, Godslayer. You are not alone."

Want to be notified when sequels are released? Register as a Citizen at hellsongseries.com

Need to look up a term?
Check out the Gehennic Encyclopedia as a free download on Kindle or view at our website: hellsongseries.com/encyclopedia

Hellsong Series

EVEN HELL HAS KNIGHTS

HELLSONG BOOK 1

Shaun McCoy

"McCoy writes with a passion for action."
—Bonnie Blanard, Author of Master of Westfall Plantation

What is it like to be damned?

Arturus knows.

Born in Hell, Arturus has never had the chance to meet his creator or seek redemption; but that doesn't mean he has no destiny. He lives near the village of Harpsborough, whose people have torn a moment of peace from the unwilling claws of damnation—and damnation wants it back.

Future omens are poor. Infidels roam the wilds, devils are amassing, and the very stones of Hell themselves have begun to break apart. But even while they fight damnation, Arturus and the hunters of Harpsborough find themselves facing off against traitors from amongst their own ranks and a people they thought they'd left far behind.

Look for *Even Hell Has Knights* and continue exploring the Hellsong Universe!

Hellsong Series

Like a character? Want to follow them through the Hellsong universe?

Cris returns in *Wasteland*.

Cris appears in *Even Hell Has Knights* and *March till Death*.

El Cid, Q and Aiden appear in *Knight of Gehenna* and *March till Death*

A Note from Sipub

Did you enjoy this book? If you did, please keep in mind that we are a small press. Sisyphean Publishing does not have the marketing dollars to match a "big five" or mainstream publisher. We rely on you, our reader, to spread the word about our amazing tales.

So if you would, take a moment to leave a review at your relevant point of sale, share your thoughts about this novel with a friend, and/or make the appropriate sacrifice/propitiation/prayer to your deity of choice (except for *Kurtulmak*, that would just be awkward) on our behalf!

Sincerely,

Michael Cannon
Director of Distribution
Sisyphean Publishing

Shaun McCoy lives in South Carolina. He is an
accomplished Pianist, Cage Fighter, Chess Player
and Writer. You can check out his fan page at
www.facebook.com/shaunomccoy